A *Spur of the Moment*
Proposition . . .

Mischief sparkled in the depths of his dark brown eyes as he inched closer to her. "Call in sick tomorrow."

"No!"

"Why not?"

"Because I'm not sick, that's why not."

"Come on, Candy. Take a day off and play hooky with me."

She looked at him as if he had suddenly sprouted horns. "No!"

"I'll bet you a home-cooked dinner that by this time tomorrow night, after you've spent the whole day with me, you'll have had more fun than you've had in a long time."

"Nice try, Nick, but the answer is still no."

"What if I promise not to touch you? I won't lay a hand on you."

His hands, she recalled vividly, were too clever, too quick, and once they started moving, she knew she wouldn't have the emotional or physical wherewithal to stop them.

"No."

But even Candace could hear the lack of conviction in her tone . . .

Berkley Books by Sarah G. Joseph

WEDDING BELLS: WITH THIS RING
WEDDING BELLS: TO LOVE AND TO CHERISH

WEDDING BELLS

To Love and to Cherish

A novel by

Sarah G. Joseph

B

BERKLEY BOOKS, NEW YORK

WEDDING BELLS: TO LOVE AND TO CHERISH

A Berkley Book / published by arrangement with the author

PRINTING HISTORY
Berkley edition / September 1991

ISBN: 0-425-12896-2

A BERKLEY BOOK ® TM 757,375
Berkley Books are published by The Berkley Publishing Group,
200 Madison Avenue, New York, New York 10016.
The name "Berkley" and the "B" logo are trademarks belonging to
Berkley Publishing Corporation.

PRINTED IN THE UNITED STATES OF AMERICA

10 9 8 7 6 5 4 3 2 1

To the memory of
Betty Henrichs
most beloved friend.
We miss you, Betty.

To Love
and to
Cherish

1

WATER LAPPED AGAINST THE SIDES OF *the gondola as it floated down a narrow canal in Venice, beneath ancient stone bridges, beside towering spires of cathedrals. Candace lazily lifted her arm, resting her hand on the side of the boat. She smiled at the man who poled them down the byway, his broad shoulders looking even broader beneath his striped gondolier's shirt, a white lacy garter bound about his arm, his white teeth gleaming, his black hair . . .*

Wait a minute. Black hair?

Candace wrenched herself out of her daydream, managing to ignore all the chaos that went on around her. Don didn't have black hair. Medium brown, yes, but not black. And his shoulders weren't broad, either. Never in a million years would he have broad shoulders like the man in her daydream. Not unless he started working out at a gym, which was highly unlikely, knowing Don the way she did. His idea of exercise was to flick through the TV channels with his remote control.

Change locales, she told herself, and gazing off, focusing on the grimy coffeepot that sat on a nearby table, she put herself back into the daydream.

The Thames.

Oh, yeah, that's a good one, she decided.

The Thames. A sleek little punt skimming through the water. Oaks older than Queen Elizabeth I stood guard by the river as willows draped their wispy limbs into the water.

Candace lounged at one end of the boat, wearing a frothy pink Edwardian frock and white kidskin high-button shoes, a frilly parasol protecting her fragile porcelain complexion from the gentle English sun. At the other end of the boat stood a man in white linen trousers. From Savile Row? Yes, definitely from Savile Row. His white shirt sleeves were rolled up to the elbow, a lacy white garter about his upper arm, exposing dark-skinned, muscular forearms.

He smiled at her, his white teeth gleaming, thick lashes barely concealing his black eyes that glistened with desire. . . .

Not again, Candace thought, coming out of her daydream to the harsh reality around her. Don didn't have black eyes. His were kind of a hazel-green color. And he definitely didn't have thick lashes.

Who was this guy who kept invading her daydream, anyhow? She wanted to think about Don, the guy she loved, or if not loved, the guy she really liked a whole lot. She didn't want to fantasize about some dark-haired, dark-eyed muscle-bound guy with lots of hair on his arms and chest and lashes any woman in her right mind would kill for.

Chest? How did she know her daydream invader had hair on his chest?

Of course, it only stood to reason. If he had hairy forearms, he would have to have a hairy chest. And that could only mean one thing—she hadn't been thinking about Don. His chest was baby-bottom smooth. And pale. Very pale. Almost anemic.

Give it up, McFarren, she told herself, and with a heavy sigh looked down at her steno pad. Occasionally as she had daydreamed she had doodled, her fingers adding a visual life to her fantasy. But now as she peered at the lines and squiggles, she couldn't figure out just what exactly she had drawn. It looked sort of like a face. But whose? Certainly not Don's. The face on the pad was more angular than Don's, with a squarer chin and much stronger nose, one that seemed to come to life and breathe on its own.

Too bad she was so lousy at sketching. Maybe if she had more of a talent at it, she would know who she had been thinking about, who had invaded her private fantasy. Despite the unpracticed scrawl, the subject looked pretty good.

Studying her drawing again, looking at it more closely, she began to get an uneasy feeling inside. The nose, the thick lashes, the jaw . . .

No, it couldn't be him. Not Nick Giulianni. She had banished him from her thoughts a couple of months ago, shortly after Elise and Tony's wedding. And she hadn't thought of him since then, either.

You've just had a mere slip of the mind, sort of like a slip of the tongue, she told herself, reshelving Nick Giulianni to far recesses of her memory where he rightfully belonged. It really didn't matter who she had drawn, whose face had appeared on the steno pad before her. What mattered was that she should have been paying closer attention to the meeting now going on around her, taking notes instead of doodling, daydreaming, dredging up memories of the past. Because that's all Nick Giulianni was. A memory. Nothing more, nothing less. And she would have been more than happy to take notes if anyone in the room would only say something important enough for her to jot down. But as usual, no one had.

Dr. John Shaumberger, one of the R&D lab's quirky researchers, was having another one of his lengthy arguments over computer-chip capacity with Dr. Hector Pritchet, John's so-called partner. From Candace's point of view, theirs was less a partnership than a constant clash of personalities and opposing opinions. The two men had never gotten along, even when they were in full agreement.

She glanced over at Dr. Marcus Franklin, head of R&D, in hopes of catching his attention. But after one or two subtle gestures on her part—a slight wave of her pencil, a quiet clearing of her throat—Candace gave up. She wouldn't receive any help from him. He seemed absolutely mesmerized by what his genius underlings were saying. Or, rather, what they were shouting at each other.

Well, she had better things to do. Instead of sitting there in the R&D division's designated meeting room that had the square footage of a large broom closet, wasting time listening to John and Hector rant and rave, she could be back at her desk, transcribing the scientists' often untranscribable notes or catching up on her filing. Anything but sitting there, doing nothing. Anything to get off work a little closer to five o'clock than her usual 6:30. It was her birthday, for heaven's sake.

But it looked as though she wouldn't be getting off at quitting time today. Experience with this brainy bunch told Candace as much. Once John and Hector got their tongues and egos all wound up, it could take them hours to settle down, their spleens finally vented. And Dr. Franklin—good old Dr. Franklin—wouldn't do a thing to stop them. He never did. "Creative minds need purging occasionally," was his excuse for allowing arguments like this one to continue.

Creative minds, Candace thought, shaking her head. Well, John and Hector were creative, all right, but they were also strange. Very strange. With the exception of herself, every person on the six-man research team was exactly like the other—highly gifted in matters of science and technology, but downright weird where aspects of normal life were concerned. Only the color and length of their hair and their uniquely odd clothes distinguished one from another. Each of them, even Dr. Susan Hardesty, the team's sole female researcher, lived in their own little world of slide rules, test tubes, and mathematical equations.

And what kind of world do you live in, Candy, my dear? Candace asked herself.

One of reality, she hoped. One where common sense and stability always took precedence over flights of fancy and wild, rash behavior. But occasionally she had to wonder, especially after spending eight, sometimes ten hours a day with this collection of oddballs, whose IQs were in the high triple-digit range. Perhaps that had been the cause of her wild, rash behavior with Nick that night two months ago. No stable person in control of her emotions, no person using common sense, would have done what she had done.

Minutes later, the argument between John and Hector continued unabated, seemingly with no end in sight. Candace glanced up at the door and saw Shelly Woods's face in the small glass pane. Shelly gestured at her, telling her in a strange form of sign language that she wanted to talk to her.

For a response, Candace managed an almost imperceptible shrug and let her eyes dart around the room. Shelly, understanding that she couldn't get away immediately, merely nodded.

After another hour of listening to the irate researchers bash each other's credibility, Dr. Franklin finally called the meeting to an end. Grateful to be free of the canteen's headache-inducing atmosphere, Candace hurried out into the hall, bypassing the usual route to her office in favor of seeking out Shelly.

"Rough meeting?" Shelly asked as Candace stopped before her desk.

"Rough? No, frustrating is more like it. I don't understand why Dr. Franklin calls these weekly meetings in the first place. We never accomplish anything. They're always the same, week in, week out. The minute one of the researchers starts to update the others on his or her progress, somebody invariably jumps in and tells him how wrong, how absolutely implausible his theory is. The six of them are supposed to be a team, individuals working as one, but I'll tell you, Shelly, you'll never get me to believe it."

"If I were as dissatisfied as you seem to be," Shelly said, "I'd ask for a transfer."

"A transfer?"

"Sure, why not? I know at least a half a dozen execs here in the plant who would kill to have you as their secretary. You're always on time, you're fast and accurate—"

"Nah, I couldn't transfer out of R and D."

"Yeah, you could."

"No, I couldn't. I like the work."

"But what about that collection of weirdos?"

"Well, yeah, they can be a little hard to take at times, but basically I'm pretty happy."

Noting the puzzled frown that formed on Shelly's face, Candace knew it was time to change the subject. "What did you want to see me about?"

"See you? Oh, yeah. I almost forgot." Shelly's confused expression evolved into a grin. "Somebody sent you a big bouquet of balloons."

"Balloons?"

"Yeah."

"Are you sure they're for me?"

"Your name was on the lips of the delivery boy. I took them into your office and tied them to the back of your chair. They're gorgeous, Candy. Great big things with curly ribbons holding them together. One even has a teddy-bear-shaped balloon inside it."

"Who on earth would send me balloons?"

"I don't know. I looked for a card, but I couldn't find one."

Don, Candace thought, feeling herself grow soft and mellow inside. He had known it was her birthday, and when his company had sent him out of town on business again, he had sent her a bouquet of balloons. To let her know that he was thinking of her, that he hadn't forgotten, she decided.

"Oh, how sweet," she said. And how very untypical of him.

Shelly arched an eyebrow. "You know who sent them?"

"I've got a pretty good idea."

"That guy you've been dating, what's-his-name?"

Smiling, Candace nodded. "Don."

"Yeah, that's right—Don. Is he planning to take you some place special tonight?"

"I only wish he could."

"What's the matter, is he sick or something?"

"No, he's out of town on business."

"Whoa, what a bummer."

"Yeah, but it's okay. I'm sure he'll make up for missing tonight when he gets back to Dallas. Dinner, dancing or a movie." Maybe even an engagement ring, she thought. Nothing too extravagant, just something pretty and noticeable. Yeah, an engagement ring would be very nice.

"Sounds pretty serious."

It could be. Candace reflected over the last two years that she had dated Don. Two years of dinners and movies and pleasant but somehow not very satisfying good-night kisses at her front door. There had never been any groping in the front seat of his car, no wild surges of passion like she had experienced with—

Stop it! she told herself, feeling an unwanted resurgence in her memories of Nick and their one episode together that had left her riddled with guilt for weeks, as well as feeling oddly empty inside. Stop thinking about him. It's no use. He's gone back to New York, where he belongs. Your one night with him meant nothing, either to you or to him. The sooner you realize that, McFarren, the better off you'll be. He's out of your life for good now.

Out of her life, certainly, but obviously not out of her thoughts. Even though Nick was over a thousand miles away from her, living it up in the wild Big Apple, he still had the power to fill her with shame over what they had done—what he had talked her in to doing by simply looking at her, seducing her with his soft baritone voice, gently caressing her . . .

"Is something the matter?" Shelly asked, watching the wide range of emotions that played across Candace's face.

"Matter?" Candace shelved thoughts of Nick to the back of her mind and snapped back to the present. "Oh, no. Of course not. Everything's fine."

"Are you sure? 'Cause it looked to me like you—"

"It's probably just hunger," Candace inserted with a casual shrug. "Low blood sugar, you know. I'm starved. I only had a salad for lunch, and it was a little one at that."

Back at her desk, minutes later, Candace felt like crying when she saw the bunch of brightly colored balloons tied to the back of her chair. Although each was different, they all relayed the same message—*Happy Birthday* and *Congratulations*.

Too bad they hadn't come with a card. She would like to have seen Don's handwriting, his personal signature. It would have given his gesture so much more meaning.

Reality, however, told her that sending along a personalized card probably hadn't been possible for him. More than likely, he had gone into a florist shop in Des Moines, where he was currently attending to company business, and wired them to her office, knowing she would be there instead of at home.

How so untypically sweet of him, she thought. After dating for two years, he had finally remembered her birthday.

Suddenly another thought registered.

Maybe Don hadn't sent the balloons at all. Maybe someone else had. But who?

Not her parents. Now divorced and living with their

current spouses in different areas of the country, they always sent her separate cards, and sometimes some money, when they could afford it.

Not Elise. She had phoned early that morning from New York, before Candace had left for work. Hearing her old friend sing "Happy Birthday" long-distance had brightened her day considerably.

Candace strongly suspected that Courtney hadn't sent her the balloons, either. Good old Court tended to be a little more lavish in her gift giving, treating Candace to brunch, lunch, or dinner, whatever her busy schedule would allow.

And Candace knew for a fact that the balloons hadn't come as a collective gift from the researchers. Although she had worked with them for three years, they could barely remember her name, so a birthday gift was really out of the question.

Driving home late that afternoon with the hot late-spring Texas sunshine pouring through her car windows, Candace thought back to Valentine's Day, just two months earlier, when Elise and Tony had been married. It had been one of those picture-perfect affairs that almost all girls, little or big, dream of having. Flowers, champagne, smiling, laughing guests, a wedding dress Princess Di or Fergie would surely have gushed over, and a groom with love overflowing in his eyes.

Magic, she mused. The whole wedding had been magic from start to finish.

When Elise had called her that morning, Candace had perceived her to be ecstatically happy. That fact alone made Candace feel very good inside, very hopeful, because for a while she'd had every reason to believe that the wedding wouldn't take place. Elise and Tony had

had problems, big ones to them at the time, but they had managed to overcome them. And that proved to her that when a couple had love, true love, going for them, they could overcome just about anything.

Too bad we all can't be as lucky at love, she thought, experiencing a niggle of envy within herself. Finding a soul mate, one man who was eager and willing to commit himself to a relationship completely, was proving to be almost next to impossible, for her at least. A couple of years ago, when she had first met Don, she had thought he was the one, her soul mate, the man with whom she would spend the rest of her life. But now she was beginning to have her doubts.

Maybe the problems she and Don had lay in the fact that they were too much alike, too comfortable together, that they got along too well. Of late, when they were together, there never seemed to be any sparks between them; they never argued or even disagreed. Of course, they had never done that, even at the beginning of their relationship. From the very beginning, they had been like a pair of old shoes around each other, well-worn and just plain boring.

"No, not boring," she muttered, realizing that she had been putting Don down. "Stable and secure. Set in his ways." And there was nothing bad about that.

If anyone was boring, it was she. And if that were the case, it would explain why Don never tried to put the make on her, seduce her, get her into bed. Perhaps he no longer found her exciting enough.

"A great new method of birth control, and I'm the one who discovered it. I walk into a room, and instead of turning guys on, I put them to sleep."

But who needed that kind of life? Always fighting off men and their unwanted advances, always having the burden of being the center of attention.

"Yeah, some burden. Oh, well . . ."

If there was nothing new to watch on cable, she thought as she drove through the electric security gates of her apartment complex and pulled into an empty slot near her building, she faced another excitement-filled evening of microwaved leftovers and TV reruns.

No, damn it, not tonight, Candace decided. It was her twenty-seventh birthday. She was going to treat herself to something different, something special. Instead of the microwaved leftovers she had planned to eat, she would have dinner out. And she wouldn't simply pick up a Big Mac at the drive-through, either. She would have an honest-to-goodness sit-down dinner inside a restaurant. And afterward, if she felt like it, she might even catch a movie. Really go all out. So what if she got home after midnight and couldn't function at her usual one-hundred-percent capacity the next day at work. Big deal. She deserved a little change of pace.

Her footsteps grew lighter, more determined, as she climbed the two long flights of stairs to the building's third floor, her bouquet of beribboned balloons bobbing brightly over her blond head. A pleasant breeze greeted her as she headed for her door, elevating her spirits even more. She would go in, shower, change into something comfortable but tastefully elegant, and then head for lower Greenville Avenue and Dallas's restaurant row. Who knew, in her frame of mind, she might even turn a few young upwardly mobile males' heads.

And then she saw them, sitting in front of her door, blocking her path, and she felt like crying.

Roses. Big fat red ones in a beautiful cut-glass vase.

Looping the balloons around her arm so they wouldn't float away, she knelt down and plucked the card out of the florist's pick. Her name and address, she saw, had been scrawled on the outside of the envelope in a hand she didn't recognize. Probably the florist had written it, not the sender, she decided, opening the envelope and pulling out the small card inside.

Although I can only be with you in spirit tonight, you're always in my thoughts.
Happy Birthday.

N.

N.? Candace frowned. She didn't know anybody whose first name started with—

But she did, and the knowledge had her grabbing for the door frame to keep her balance so she wouldn't go sprawling backward onto her rear end.

N. could only be one person. Nick Giulianni.

2

EMPTY MOVING BOXES AND CARTONS stood in a haphazard pile by the kitchen door. Small appliances covered the countertops and table, waiting for Nick to find them a permanent home.

"Yeah, home," he muttered above the rock music that blared from his stereo in the living room. He glanced around and saw a strange kind of starkness to the house that he had leased. In New York, his things had filled his loft almost to capacity. Yet here in Dallas, his living quarters resembled those of someone just starting out with the bare necessities, not someone who had been on his own for almost twenty years. But that, he supposed, was just one of the many differences between living in New York and Dallas.

The thought of all that he had left behind him in New York made him shake his head in dismay. If someone had told him two years ago—no, two months ago—that he would be living in a three-bedroom house in a quiet residential neighborhood in east Dallas instead of his slightly cramped studio/loft apartment in Greenwich Village, he would have called them certifiably crazy. He was a native New Yorker, a denizen of the Big Apple and proud of it, not some laid-back Texan with a slow, easy drawl. Yet here he was, standing in the middle of the kitchen of his newly leased abode, his bags unpacked, his studio set up in one of the bedrooms, his office set up in another, just like he was planning to stay for a while, but wondering if he had done the right thing.

He had to have been out of his mind, moving to this particular neighborhood. He should have leased a condo or a loft in Deep Ellum or the West End, where the constant flurry of activity helped to generate creative ideas, not a quiet residential area, where brains tended to turn to mush over such mundane problems as keeping a lawn mowed, hedges clipped, and crabgrass controlled. What did he know about such things? He was an ex-advertising executive from Madison Avenue, used to living in places where there was no grass, only asphalt. He was a guy who had been responsible for putting scores of product slogans and jingles in the minds and on the lips of everyone across the United States, a guy who had made million-dollar deals over lunch at Le Cirque, Lutece, or the Four Seasons, a guy who had made a seven-figure salary his last year until that ulcer-inducing rat race had forced him to go out on his own and become a free-lancer, and a successful one at that.

"Face it, Giulianni, you may have made a big mistake by coming here."

He must have been out of his mind, all right, he decided as he opened a cabinet door and began shoving appliances inside, letting their cords hang out in a tangled mess. Either out of his mind, or there was something far more serious wrong with him. Like momentarily going weak in the head. Or, better still, going weak in the knees at the sight of a well-stacked, blond, blue-eyed woman.

No, he couldn't blame Candace; she hadn't been the entire cause of his behavior, just part of it. He had needed a change of scenery. For ten years he had lived in the same Greenwich Village loft, had seen the same old faces in the neighborhood, heard the same old stories, dealt with the same group of cutthroats on Madison Avenue that had turned him sour in the first place. Life had grown so boring and predictable that when his brother Tony had called him from Dallas to tell him that he was getting married, Nick had jumped at the chance to get away. He had told himself that acting as Tony's best man was a surefire way for him to take a badly needed break, and that Dallas was as good a place as any to relax. And relax he had.

He had heard stories, read magazine articles, and seen film footage in movies and on TV of the sprawling north-central Texas city, but nothing had prepared him for actually experiencing it up close and personal. From the first moment he had stepped out of the plane onto the concourse at DFW, he had felt calmer, less pressured. The people he had met seemed friendlier, more open, more welcoming. And for reasons he couldn't explain, he'd had an immediate hankering to go to the nearest western-wear store and buy himself a Stetson hat and a pair of cowboy boots. What was the old saying? ''When in Rome . . .'' Well, the same went for Texas.

Even the weather had helped to lighten his mood. He'd left Manhattan 2 months ago, covered in snow and bitter icy winds that had blown down the concrete-and-glass canyons, chilling him right to the bone. By comparison, the mild early-February winter Dallas experienced had seemed almost balmy. There was Dallas's laid-back life-style to consider, too. Oh, it had its usual rush-hour traffic jams and its long lines at the theaters, sports events, rock concerts, and supermarkets, but all in all, it didn't come close to being as nerve-racking as New York's.

And then he'd met Candace—tall, blond, sexy as sin, sweet Candy McFarren—and everything had changed. His attitude, his outlook on life, his goals. Even now, months after the fact, he could still recall how he had reacted, how he had felt when he first saw her.

He had been in Tony's kitchen, searching through his brother's nearly bare cupboards for something to eat or drink, when Candace and Elise, then Tony's fiancée and now his bride, had arrived. Chances were, if he had been in the room when she'd walked in, he would have drooled and jabbered like some acned adolescent suffering from a major hormonal overload, sweaty palms, heart pounding like a jackhammer, tongue tied. Instead, when he'd heard her voice and been intrigued by it, he'd taken the time to collect his wits and prepare himself. A good thing, too, because one look at her and he'd actually felt his knees begin to buckle; she had been that breathtaking.

But seeing her was nothing compared with the privilege he'd had of talking to her, getting to know her, discovering the enormous degree of intelligence she possessed and, for reasons known only to her, tried to keep hidden. Looking at her, however, was just the tip of the iceberg. His internal masculine system had undergone a tremendous trial later that evening as he sat beside her in the booth of the Mexican restaurant to which they had gone, smelling her perfume, feeling the heat of her body radiate out to his.

At one point during their first evening together, he had gotten a strong image of himself as a prehistoric caveman, throwing Candy over his shoulder and carrying her off to his lair, to keep her hidden so that others of his gender could never cast their eyes on her again. The fact that he had wanted her with such intensity continued to astound him even now. He had never felt that way about a woman before, neither his two ex-fiancées, whom he had loved or, at the time, thought he loved, or any of the other women he had met, dated, and/or bedded.

While "sexy as sin" did come very close, it still didn't describe Candace adequately. There was something about her, something intangible that Nick could neither name nor define that had made him act oddly and feel reckless when he was around her, when he thought of her.

"Yeah, odd and reckless—that about sums you up," he mumbled, giving a disparaging shake of his head as he slammed the cabinet door closed. "You're either entering into an early mid-life crisis, or you're getting all weirded out."

He dismissed the mid-life crisis theory. At thirty-five he hardly considered himself middle-aged. He would be there in a few more years, perhaps, but he wasn't there yet. His second theory, however, he could buy without a qualm. "Weirded out" was about the best explanation he could come up with. After all, he had left his home, his friends, the business contacts that he had worked so hard to accumulate, and had traveled well over a thousand miles to a strange city to start over. If that wasn't weird, he'd like to know what was.

But in spite of his rash move to Dallas, he still had goals. And the first of those was to start his own advertising firm. Here he could work for and possibly attain that dream; in New York, he would never have been able to come close to seeing it through to fruition. The competition on Madison Avenue was too fierce. And this time, being the man in charge of operations instead of merely being a hired underling, he would see that it was run with a high degree of ethics. Backstabbing and taking credit where credit wasn't due would not be allowed in his place of business. That sort of thing had happened to him one too many times in the past, and he simply wouldn't allow it. If and when he ever learned of an employee accepting recognition or praise for another's hard labor, that employee would be out on his butt in a minute.

And his second goal . . .

"Candy, sweet Candy," he whispered, getting a crystal-clear image of her in his mind, her pale blond hair draped about her shoulders like a golden shawl, her blue eyes wide with eagerness, intelligence, and, oddly enough, innocence. Oh, to be able to see those eyes filled once again with desire and then to watch them grow sleepy with satisfaction. To be able to have her return the words and the sentiment that he had spoken to her their one night together.

But with thoughts of Candace came thoughts of another—Don, Candy's so-called boyfriend. Nick grimaced and shook his head.

He might not know Don very well, but he wasn't exactly a total stranger, either; they had met the night of Tony and Elise's wedding. And Nick's first impression of Don had been that Don was more of a convenience for Candace than a lover with serious intentions.

Oh, Don had seemed nice enough on the surface, if a little self-absorbed, but something had been missing, something closely akin to ordinary affection or good old basic chemistry, because Don and Candace just hadn't looked right together. She was slightly taller than he, for one thing, and for another, Don hadn't once offered to dance with her, even though Nick had heard her suggest it. And Nick knew that a guy who was in love, or deeply "in like," with a good-looking woman would never miss the opportunity to hold her. But not Don. No, Don hadn't wanted to be bothered. Even later, as Nick watched the two of them from a distance, he had noticed Don go out of his way to avoid so much as touching Candace. He had sat beside her and listened to what she'd had to say, all the time looking a little bored, but never once during the course of the evening had he put his arm around her or held her hand. The guy acted more like an older brother who had been coerced into going to the wedding with his little sister than a man with his lover.

Nick decided that starting his own advertising firm and making a success of it would be a breeze compared with convincing Candace to dump Don, her so-called boyfriend of two years. He may not have known her for very long, only a few days as a matter of fact, but it didn't take a lifetime for him to realize that she was the kind of lady who did things by the book, so to speak, that she lived her life according to a strict set of codes. He had no argument with that; he liked to think that he lived his own life by a set of codes. But Candace's ethics almost bordered on excessive suppression, as if someone in her past had told her that she wouldn't be loved or accepted if she veered from the straight and narrow even the slightest bit. He figured out that much when she had gone all stiff and icy on him after they had slept together on their first date.

And what a mistake that had been, Nick mused as he headed out of the kitchen and into the front hall to answer the knock at his door. It had been a joyous encounter, certainly, one that he would never forget for as long as he lived, but it had been a mistake, nevertheless. Candace had been so mortified by what they had done that she had almost burst into tears when their breathing settled back to normal. He had tried to console her, of course, convince her that it was all right, that what they had done was natural and safe and nothing to be ashamed of. But she had insisted that he leave her apartment. Not knowing what else to do, he had gone, alternately cursing himself all the way back to his brother's apartment and trying to figure out a way to see her again.

Nick shoved thoughts of Candace and the past to the back of his mind and opened the door. A young man stood on the porch, the evening sun setting slowly behind him.

"Mr. Giulianni?"

The young man extended his right hand, and Nick took it, thinking that the voice sounded familiar.

"Yes."

"I'm Toby Singleton. I called you earlier about the ad you ran in the paper? You are still looking for an artist, I hope. I mean, you haven't filled the position yet, have you?"

Nick arched a eyebrow in surprise. From the brief conversation they had had earlier that day, he had gotten the distinct impression that Toby was older, more mature, more experienced. But looking at him now, he realized that Toby was just a kid, no older than nineteen or twenty, and probably still in school.

"No, the position is still open," he said. "Come on in. Get out of this heat."

"Thank you." Toby stepped inside the house, letting Nick close the door. "I know that showing up this way, out of the blue, is probably an inconvenience for you, but I couldn't wait. I wanted to show you some of my drawings before you had a chance to give the job to somebody else. Before I chickened out, too, to be honest. Have you interviewed many others ahead of me?''

Nick laughed at the young man's exuberance. Toby reminded him of how excited he'd been on his first job interview. It seemed that while times may have changed, young people were still young people.

"No, as a matter of fact, you're the first, so relax, okay?"

He waved a hand at the sofa against the wall. "Have a seat. Make yourself comfortable. I would offer you something to drink, but as you can see I'm still moving in. I just got to the kitchen boxes tonight, and I haven't had a chance to go to the supermarket yet."

"Oh, that's all right. I'm not thirsty."

The fact that Toby kept licking his lips told Nick that the boy had just lied. But that was okay; Nick understood. On his first job interview he'd gotten a case of nervous "dry mouth," too.

"Okay, Toby. While I look at your portfolio why don't you fill me in a little on your background?"

"My background?"

"That's right."

"Well, okay. Er, I'm black, healthy, still live with my parents. . . ."

"No, not that kind of background. I'm talking about your work credentials." Seeing the confused look continue to linger on Toby's face, he added, "What kind of experience do you have?"

Toby swallowed. "I'm afraid I don't have a lot, sir. At the moment I'm, uh, sort of the resident cartoonist on my school paper."

Nick grinned. "And what school would that be?"

"Eastfield Community College, out in Mesquite.

That's just southeast of here.''

Hearing the deflation of enthusiasm in Toby's voice made Nick nod. ''I see.'' The one thing he didn't need starting out was inexperienced help. But that didn't compare with possibly bruising a young man's ego. It must have taken a lot of courage for Toby to come over tonight. ''So, how's the paper doing?''

''Okay, I guess.''

''Does it sell a lot of copies?''

''No, sir, as a matter of fact, it doesn't sell any at all. The paper's free of charge to all the students.'' Toby brightened a little, some of his former enthusiasm returning. ''But my journalism teacher says that it's my cartoons that make us always run out of copies.''

''How often is it published?''

''Every other week. And it's not just my journalism teacher who says that, either. Students and other teachers are always coming up to me in the halls, telling me how much they like what I've done.''

Flipping through the pages of Toby's dog-eared sketch pads, Nick could see why the young man got such high praises. He was a very good artist, though obviously still unschooled in the some of the more sophisticated areas of the craft.

''Do you do anything else besides cartoons?''

''Well, yeah. I've done a few paintings. Some in oils, but mostly in acrylics. You know, the usual classroom stuff, still lifes and landscapes. No portraits. I'm not ready for that yet, but I'm working on it. One day I hope to become an artist.''

''Looks to me like you already are.'' Nick closed the last sketch pad and handed it back to Toby. ''Those are very impressive.''

''You think so?''

"I know so. How old are you?"

"Twenty," Toby said. "I'll be twenty-one in July."

Nick leaned forward, resting his elbows on his knees as he turned his head to study Toby. "It may be out of line for me to ask this, but I'd like to know something."

"What's that, sir?"

"Why aren't you at RISD, instead of a simple community college?"

"RISD?"

"Rhode Island School of Design," Nick said.

Toby issued a humorless chuckle. "Besides never having heard of it, until you just now mentioned it, I don't have the money, sir. My folks don't have any, either."

Nick understood completely. Coming from a big Italian family, he had been in Toby's shoes himself at one time. His father's paycheck had only gone so far, covering the basic necessities like food, housing, and clothing; there just hadn't been enough for him, or any of the others, to attend a good school. And even with the scholarship he'd won, he'd still been forced into taking odd jobs to make ends meet.

"Yeah," Nick said, "I know where you're coming from."

"It takes just about every penny my mom and dad make to keep a roof over our heads. See, I've got three younger brothers at home."

"I had one younger brother and three younger sisters."

"Then you do know what I'm talking about."

"I'll bet you've got a part-time job, don't you?"

"Yeah. I fry hamburgers and french fries."

"I worked in a deli."

"It pays okay, I guess, but I barely make enough for my tuition and art supplies."

Nick nodded. "No chance, I suppose, of you getting a scholarship?"

Looking somewhat crestfallen, Toby merely shook his head. "My grades weren't good enough. Art is the only thing I'm really good at. To get a scholarship to a good school you've got to make better than Cs in English and math, and I had to work my tail off just to get that."

"Well, where your art is concerned, you're better than good. And don't ever let anybody tell you differently."

Toby beamed. "Thank you, sir."

"Don't thank me yet. You've still got a long way to go. But I figure with the proper guidance and a little hands-on training there's every possibility that you could turn into a first-rate illustrator."

"You think so?"

"I know so, Toby."

"Well, I've always thought that myself, but where am I gonna get a break like that? Nobody'll hire me 'cause I don't have any experience, and I can't get the experience I need 'cause nobody'll hire me. I know, I've been looking for months."

"The old Catch twenty-two scenario."

"I guess," Toby said with a heavy sigh. "I don't know what a 'Catch twenty-two' scenario is."

Nick laughed as he stood up. "I'll explain it to you one day."

Toby's eyes widened slowly. "You will? I mean, are you saying that I've got the job?"

"Yeah, that's what I'm saying. Of course, I can't pay you a whole lot at first. A buck over minimum wage is about all I can manage right now. I'm sort of working on a shoestring myself."

"Hey, no problem. I can handle that. It'll be more than I'm making now."

"So when can you start? Would tomorrow be too soon?"

"Tomorrow?"

"Yeah, why not? Unless you've got something else planned."

Toby leaped to his feet. "No, tomorrow's fine."

"When's your last class?"

"Eleven. I get out at noon, and I can be here by one, if the buses are running on time."

"I'll see you at one, then."

"I got the job," Toby muttered to himself in jubilant disbelief as Nick saw him out the front door.

Laughing, Nick closed the door. "Yeah, you got it, all right."

Hiring a kid full of talent and ambition but who had no experience may have been a little reckless on his part, and not what he had originally intended, but Nick didn't regret having made the offer. It would give him the chance to mold Toby and guide him, teach him everything he knew. Maybe even learn something himself in the process.

Reckless, Nick thought. There it was again, that word that described his actions so often here of late.

"You must be getting soft in your old age, Giulianni."

But maybe getting soft was what he needed right now. He'd spent too many years being a hard-edged son of a bitch on Madison Avenue. Maybe he needed to get in touch with his beginnings, see a reflection of the bright-eyed innocent young man he'd once been before the dog-eat-dog world of advertising had gotten to him and jaded him, turned him sour.

And maybe by becoming softer, more understanding, he would stand a better chance with Candace. He certainly hoped so.

At the thought of Candace, he wondered what her reaction had been when the balloons were delivered to her office. Better yet, what had gone through her mind when she saw the flowers waiting outside her apartment door and read the card attached.

She had probably been stunned, he decided. She hadn't heard from him in two months—not because he hadn't thought of her, or wanted to call or write her, but mainly because he'd been much too busy to get in touch with her. He'd had the move from Manhattan to Dallas to contend with. And then there had been his business to set up, his house to put in order.

All that kept him from going to her now and celebrating her birthday with her was the gnawing belief that she needed some time to get used to the fact that he was back in her life and that, regardless of what she felt for good old Don, he intended to be a part of it. Their first encounter had assured him of that much. He couldn't think about it and not want more. Once with Candy, sweet Candy, just wasn't enough.

But their second encounter wouldn't be a spur-of-the-moment action as their first had been. The second, and all the encounters they had after it, would be different, more meaningful. His days of being "Love 'em and leave 'em" Nick Giulianni were over.

3

COURTNEY STEPPED OUT OF THE
shower just as her answering machine clicked on. It was
on the desk in her office across the hall, but it sounded
like it was in the same room. She would have to remember to turn down the volume.

"Please," she muttered, wrapping the towel around
her, "don't be someone calling from the office. And
don't be a client, either."

At present, her mood didn't allow her to plunge into
some kind of heavy crisis. Her day at work, as a lot of
others here of late, had been very hectic. All she wanted
to do was eat the salad her housekeeper had left for her
in the fridge and then curl up with a good movie on
cable. She had to give her mind a chance to gear down,
or else it would turn completely to mush.

The machine beeped, ending her prerecorded message,
as she slowly made her way toward the study. She paused
just inside the doorway to flip on the switch, flooding
the small but tastefully appointed room in muted light.

"I hate this machine of yours." The sound of Candace's voice made Courtney pause. "The one time I need to talk to you, person to person, I get your dumb recording. But since you're not at home, I suppose I'll have to make do with this."

Neither the office nor a client, Courtney thought, hearing Candace take a deep breath then release it on a long sigh, but a crisis nonetheless.

"Believe it or not, I had plans made for tonight," Candace said. "Why shouldn't I? It's my birthday, right? I was going to treat myself to dinner, go out to a nice restaurant, and then take in a movie. But I didn't. In fact, I'm still at home. And you want to know why? I got flowers today. Roses. And you'll never in a million years guess who sent them to me. With the way my luck's been running lately, he probably sent the balloons, too."

Intrigued by Candace's message, Courtney tied the towel around her, tucking it in front between her breasts, and picked up the receiver, ending the recording with a push of the button. "Who?" she said.

"Court? Is that you?"

"In the flesh. And I mean that almost literally."

"Where the devil were you?"

"I just got out of the shower. So who sent you the roses and balloons? Don?"

"No. I wish he had, though." Candace paused a beat for emphasis. "Nick sent them."

Courtney grinned. "Nick?"

"Yeah. Nick Giulianni. You remember him, don't you? Tall guy, broad shoulders, black hair down past his collar. Tony's brother? Ellie's new brother-in-law? You met him two months ago at their wedding."

"I know who he is." Courtney's grin grew broader.

Candace had left out Nick's thick eyelashes in her description. And his brown eyes that had held a very wicked gleam whenever he had looked Candace's way. Courtney didn't have to be a mind reader to know that Nick had a thing for her old friend. Lust had radiated around him like pulses from a microwave oven on full power. Probably due in fact to Candace having slept with him on their first date, she decided.

"So he sent you roses, huh?"

"That's right."

"What color?"

"Red. Long-stemmed red ones, just beginning to open from the bud. I found them outside my door, in a cut-glass vase with baby's breath and ferns."

"Ah. Red, the color of love."

"Knock it off, Court. There's no love involved here. The guy's a thousand miles away."

Courtney thought for a moment, then suggested, "Distance makes the heart grow fonder?"

"That's absence, you ninny. Absence makes the heart grow fonder, not distance."

"Well, he's both, isn't he? Absent at a great distance?"

"Yeah."

Hearing the somewhat despondent note in Candace's voice, Courtney said, "Of course, he might not have been distant at all now if you'd just given him some encouragement. He might have stuck around town for a while."

"I didn't want him to stick around. Frankly, I'm glad he left when he did. And just for your information, a guy like Nick Giulianni doesn't need encouragement. Take it from me, I know. All I did was smile at him a couple of times, let him take me out to dinner—I thought it was the nice, polite thing to do for my best friend's future brother-in-law, you know? But then he had to go and ruin the whole evening by—'' Candace broke off. "Well, you know what happened."

Courtney stifled a chuckle and shook her head. Poor Candy, she thought. Still suffering like a guilt-ridden Puritan. "Yes, I know. Nature took its course."

"Nature had nothing to do with what Nick and I did. It was pure animal lust."

The notion of telling Candace that lust was all right on certain occasions occurred to Courtney, but she decided that it probably wasn't what Candace wanted to hear right now. "Maybe so, maybe not," she said.

"On, there's no maybes about it. It was lust, pure and simple."

"What about chemistry? You are aware that there is such a thing as chemistry, aren't you? It's that rare spark that attracts two people to each other and sets off an inevitable chain reaction?"

Candace groaned. "Don't remind me. I've spent the last two months trying to forget what I did. What *we* did—Nick and I. I've been trying to forget him, too."

"Haven't had much luck at either one, though, have you?"

"I thought I had. Until today." Candace heaved a heavy sigh. "Why did he have to send me flowers and balloons? Well, the flowers, for certain. I'm not so sure about the balloons. I'm only guessing that he sent them; there wasn't a card attached."

"Candy?"

"Yeah?"

"I know this may come as a big surprise to you, but the reason he sent you those things is because he probably likes you. At least, that's how it sounds to me. I mean, if he didn't like you, he wouldn't still be thinking about you. And he wouldn't have remembered your birthday.''

"Yeah, I know. He—wait a minute. Say that again.''

"Say what?'' Courtney said.

"About him remembering my birthday. How did he know about it in the first place? And how did he know it was today? Who told him?''

"Well, I . . .''

"Court, *you* told him?''

"It could have been Ellie.''

"No, it couldn't have been her. She was too wrapped up in her own problems before the wedding to mention something as trivial as my birthday to him. You did it. You told him.''

"Okay, maybe I did. But it wasn't intentional. It must have slipped out as we were talking.''

"Talking, huh? When did you have a chance to talk with him?''

"At the wedding reception. I suppose.''

"No, not then. You and your boss, David what's-his-name, were huddled together at your table, talking about one of your cases. I know, because I overheard you. Honestly, you two didn't even dance. And it was a darn good band.''

"That's right,'' Courtney said, remembering. "David and I did spend a lot of time talking shop that night, didn't we?''

"A pretty strange thing to do, too, if you ask me. I mean, if I'd been with a good-looking guy like him, legal briefs would have been the last thing on my mind.''

"Well, you know what they say, Candy: No rest for the weary.''

"You mean 'wicked,' don't you?''

"Whatever, we just aren't able to get away from it.

Here of late, it always seems to follow us around where ever we go. I hope things will lighten up a bit when we get Mr. Bryant and his company squared away, merge it with that company out in San Francisco. Until that happens, though, I suppose it'll keep taking up an exorbitant amount of our time. Like tonight, for instance. Why, I was at the office until after seven, talking to some big corporate attorney out on San Francisco.''

"Court, put a sock in it, would you? I don't give a hoot about your Mr. Bryant or some lawyer out in San Francisco. And I'm not buying your attempt at stalling me, either. When did you tell Nick about my birthday?''

"Mmm. When did I tell him? Are you wanting to know what day?''

"Day, hour, minute—does it really matter? Just tell me.''

"Well, Candy, I suppose the only time I could have told him was—'' Courtney realized she couldn't put off the inevitable any longer; she had to tell Candace the truth, the whole truth, and nothing but. "Was when I drove him out to the airport.''

"*You* drove him?''

"Yes.''

"Why?''

"I wanted to. I thought it was the polite thing to do. Besides, I couldn't very well let him spend a small fortune taking a taxi out there, could I?''

"Why not? I would have. He's not family, or anything.''

"No, but he is a friend. A very good friend, I might add.''

"Since when?''

"Since the wedding,'' Courtney said. "Look, what's

the big deal, any way? All I did was drive him to the airport.''

At the mention of the wedding, Candace let the receiver slip slowly away from her ear, her blue eyes narrowing suspiciously as she got a clear mental image of two closely related events that happened at the wedding reception—Tony deliberately tossing Elise's garter to his brother Nick, and moments later, Elise tossing her bouquet. A crowd of single women had lined up to catch it, but Candace, believing it a silly act and a useless waste of time, had elected not to participate and stood off to one side, out of the line of fire. But Courtney—her good old devious friend Courtney—had had other ideas. When Elise turned her back to the crowd and tossed the bouquet over her head, Courtney had batted it in Candace's direction, like a professional volleyball player setting up a shot, and Candace had been forced to catch it.

The bridal bouquet, the flowers and balloons—it was all beginning to make sense to Candace. ''I'll tell you what the big deal is, Court. I get the strangest feeling that you're up to something.''

''Who, me?'' Courtney issued a nervous laugh. ''What on earth would I be up to?''

''Matchmaking, that's what.''

''Don't be ridiculous, Candy. I'm a lawyer, not a matchmaker. Besides, I don't even believe in that stuff. It's archaic and demeaning as hell.''

''Then why did you tell Nick about my birthday?''

''Because he asked me, that's why.''

''Oh, you're saying that it just came up casually in the conversation as you were driving him out to the airport?''

''That's right.''

''Hah!''

"Candy, if I didn't know better, I'd swear you were doubting my word."

"I am."

Courtney took a deep breath, striving to maintain her composure. It wouldn't do for her to break out laughing. To behave as if she were offended, she decided, was the much better route to take. "Really, this is no way to talk to an old dear and trusted friend."

"Dear, maybe, but not trusted. Not any longer. What are you trying to do to me, Court? Ruin my life?"

No, I'm trying to help you get a life, you straitlaced little prude, Courtney thought. There's a lot more to living than waiting around for some pencil-necked geek like Don Rollins to make the first move. You'll be an old woman before he ever decides to commit to a relationship that involves a marriage license and a wedding ring.

"Of course not, Candy. You're my friend, my very best friend, now that Ellie's moved away and left us alone. Besides, I love you too much to ever do something stupid like try to ruin your life."

"Then would you please stop interfering?"

"I didn't think I was. Honestly."

In truth, Courtney had only wanted to help Nick sway Candace over to his way of thinking. Or, to be perfectly blunt, to help him win her. She liked him, but just as a friend. And friends, good friends, always helped each other when they needed it. And Nick would need all the assistance he could get to break Candace out of her self-imposed shell of rigid propriety, a shell that she had been living in for almost as long as Courtney had known her. If anyone could wake up Candace and show her what she had been missing, Courtney had the feeling that it was Nick.

After all, he had already caused a crack in Candy's shell, made her act out of character by going to bed with him. Of course, it had left Candace riddled with guilt for weeks afterward, but that kind of guilt was normal, Courtney decided. Regretting doing something silly, like buying a trendy trinket on a whim in a department store and wishing you'd thought twice before buying it when you got home, was a natural way of life. Almost everybody, at one time or another, had done something slightly out of character. But *not* doing it, believing you had to be perfect all the time, was very unnatural. And that, unfortunately, was Candace.

For as long as Courtney had known her, she had always done the right thing in a public setting, making sure she made the proper response, never offending anyone, always behaving in the appropriate way. Only in the privacy of her apartment, around Courtney and Elise, her two closest friends since kindergarten, had she ever let her true character show.

In the past, before Elise had married and moved away, Candace's rapier-tongued wit had left them in stitches, literally rolling on the floor. But in public, Candace suppressed that side of her nature, preferring to behave like some kind of properly programmed windup toy, to Courtney's way of thinking. And that, more than anything, worried her. It just wasn't natural not to make a human mistake occasionally.

"Nick wanted to know when your birthday was," Courtney continued after a momentary pause, "and I told him. I didn't think it would hurt. As a matter of fact, I thought it was rather sweet of him to ask. He likes you, Candy. And you like him, too, even though I don't think you'll admit it."

"You're right, I won't. Because I don't."

In a pig's eye you don't, Courtney thought. "Then why are you getting so angry?"

"Because I've got a right to be. You'd be angry, too, if you were in my shoes. I've been going with Don for over two years now. I owe my loyalty to him, not to some smooth-talking Lothario from New York City who comes breezing into town for a few days, and then breezes right back out again. I'll probably never see Nick again, yet he sends me flowers and balloons for my birthday."

"Then if I were you," Courtney said, "I'd feel flattered as hell, and take his gifts in the manner in which I'm sure he intended them—as a compliment."

"But what about Don?"

Don again, Courtney thought. "What about him? He's not here. I'll bet he didn't even have the consideration to send you a card." She waited for Candace to contradict her spur-of-the-moment supposition, but no contradiction came. She smiled, sadly, knowing she had been right. Don hadn't sent Candace a card. Don hadn't done anything. The jerk.

"You can do better than Don, Candy, and you know it. He's not right for you."

Then who is? Candace wondered, feeling an old familiar ache swell inside of her, one that she hadn't felt since childhood, when her father and mother divorced, one that she had thought she would never to feel again. Suddenly she felt very defensive. "That's up to me to decide, don't you think?"

"Yes, you're right. It is up to you to decide. But as your friend, I think it's up to me to tell you that I hope you don't wait too long to come to your senses, to start seeing things, seeing *life*, for the way it really is, and not the way you want it to be. You're a smart girl, Candy. Much smarter than you like to let on. But that's another argument, and I don't feel like getting into it tonight.''

Deciding it was time to change her tactics, drastically, Courtney said, "Look, I'm sorry . . . for interfering, for seeming as though I'm trying to ruin your life, if that's what you truly believe.''

Candace expelled a weary sigh. "I don't, not really. I know you were only doing what you thought was best, telling me what you think. It's just that—oh, I don't know. I'm so confused right now.''

"I know you are.''

"And hurt.''

"I know that, too.'' Courtney could hear the pain in her friend's voice, and it increased her sadness, and her anger. Why couldn't Candace talk to Don this way? If she could, perhaps their relationship wouldn't be so stagnant, with Don always having the upper hand. Candace was a person, too, with wishes and dreams and desires, just like Don. Yet she always deferred to him, did things his way, no matter what the situation.

"I wanted Don to be here,'' Candace said. "I wanted to do something with him tonight. I mean, it's my birthday, damn it. He should be here.''

"Was it out-of-town business again.''

"Isn't it always?'' Candace issued a mirthless chuckle. "I'll tell you something, Court, I hope he's getting a whale of a commission check every month. He certainly deserves one, considering he's been out of town four to five days out of every seven. I don't think I've seen him but twice in the last month. No, I take that back. I've only seen him once. He phoned me between flights to let me know that he was in town but that he was heading right out again, for Atlantic City of all places. I didn't even know his sales route included New Jersey. I thought he only covered the Midwest and Rocky Mountain states.''

''The larger his route, the higher the commission possibilities,'' Courtney said.

''I know. I don't object to that, or to his being away so much. What I do object to is his company and the way they treat him, making him work so hard.''

''In today's economy he's lucky he's got a job he likes. He does like it, doesn't he?''

''I suppose. He doesn't talk much about it when we're together.'' Candace suddenly realized that, in truth, she and Don never did much of anything when they were together. A ''normal'' date for them usually consisted of dinner, either in her apartment or at a small budget-priced restaurant, and renting a video or going to a movie. Nothing extravagant, and never anything extra special or out of the ordinary, like making love. Especially making love. They had come close to it once or twice in the early days of their relationship, but there had been nothing since then. Don was always too tired, or he wasn't in the mood. He was affectionate, politely kissing her good night at her door, before he left, but he never went beyond that.

''Well, it is awfully tight out there in the private sector,'' Courtney said, interrupting Candace's private musings. ''Industrial espionage, and all that. He may not be at liberty to talk about his work. And speaking of work . . . I'd love to stay up all night and chat with you, but if I don't go to bed and get some sleep, I'm going to be a zombie at the office tomorrow.''

''Yeah, me too.''

''Happy birthday, Candy.''

''Thanks, Court.''

As Candace replaced the receiver she glanced at the

clock by her bedside. Eleven o'clock. She had spent the whole entire evening of her birthday at home, again, doing nothing.

"Well, maybe next year."

4

SATURDAY—THE ONE DAY OF THE week that Candace always looked forward to. She could sleep in late, pamper herself a little, and let her batteries recharge.

Had it been a workday, she would have been awake and out of bed by 6:30, when her alarm clock went off. But today not being a workday, she lounged around in bed, stretching and staring at the ceiling until boredom forced her out.

Bright sunlight streamed through the draped window as she made her way to the bathroom, to take care of morning's natural necessities. When she came back out again, minutes later, she glanced at the clock and groaned. "Only seven?"

The one day of the week she could sleep as late as she wanted, and she had awakened at seven. She sighed in frustration and padded into the kitchen.

But one look in the refrigerator told her that what she had already suspected was true—she needed to do some serious shopping at her nearby supermarket before the day was over. If she didn't, she wouldn't have enough to last another day. But further digging in her meager supply of food produced just enough for her to breakfast adequately on hot coffee and toast smeared with jelly.

Still wearing her fuzzy slippers and faithful old Dallas Cowboys football jersey that had an airy tear under one arm, she sat on the sofa, her feet propped up on the coffee table in front of her. A steno pad rested in her lap as she jotted down a list of "to do" things for the day.

She finished compiling her "to do" list with the addition of "dry cleaners" at the bottom of the page. Then she started on a new page, filling it with her "to buy" list. Food, personal toilet articles, household cleaning products . . .

"One day you won't ever have to do this again," she muttered. "Because one day you'll be rich and have a maid."

In her mind she conjured up an image of a rosy-cheeked woman who would not only do all her cleaning for her, but who shopped for her as well, braving the long lines at the supermarket, where toddlers always seemed to be tired and cranky, screaming at the tops of their lungs no matter what time of the day. And then her maid, this personal saint she intended to hire, would come home and put everything away in its proper place, leaving Candace with nothing to do.

"Yeah, one day, McFarren. But not today."

And not in this decade, either, from the looks of things, she decided. Until the situation changed, she would still be just an ordinary working girl, like thousands of others, struggling to make ends meet on the fixed amount of money she earned each month.

"No Prince Charming is going to come riding up on

his white stallion to rescue you from the old daily grind, kiddo.''

Outside the pages of fairy-tale books, Hollywood movie magazines, and the royal houses of Europe, she knew that Prince Charmings no longer existed. And even if they did exist, she led such a mediocre, low-profile life, they wouldn't know where to look for her to find her.

But who needed a Prince Charming? And who wanted one, anyway? This was the nineties, and she was a nineties woman. She had everything she wanted, didn't she? Intelligence, passable good looks, a reasonably good job . . . She didn't need a man. If she needed anything at all, it was a bit more drive and ambition. With that, she could be or do just about anything she wanted.

That, however, was the problem. At the ripe old age of twenty-seven, she still hadn't decided what she wanted to be when she grew up.

Being someone's wife would be nice, she mused. Being someone's mother—two or three little someones, for that matter—would be even nicer. But she would not allow herself to dwell on having the latter without having first obtained the former. Kids needed their fathers as much as they needed their mothers; she knew that much from experience.

''Cut it out, and get a move on,'' she murmured to herself. Sitting around the apartment all day daydreaming was not going to put groceries in the fridge.

Two hours later, dressed in worn faded jeans, a comfortable T-shirt, and jogging shoes, she roamed the aisles of her neighborhood supermarket, pushing her half-filled basket in front of her. Occasionally she stopped to consult her list, compare prices of the products on the shelves nearby, then either toss one in or go on to the next item.

Suddenly she had an unexplainable feeling that someone was watching her. When she looked up, what she
saw—*who* she saw—standing in front of her had her
mouth dropping open in utter surprise.

"It's amazing who you run into these days, isn't it?"
he asked with a wide friendly grin.

She hadn't heard from him in two months. Yet here
he was, standing no more than three feet from her, smiling his heart-stopping smile, just like it was a normal,
everyday occurrence.

But she wasn't going to let his crooked grin get to her
this time; it had wreaked too much havoc on her conscience once before. She hated it and him with equal
intensity. Hated the way his thick black hair parted at
one side and curled over his collar, begging for a woman's hands to comb through it. Hated the way his eyes
crinkled at the outer corners. And most of all, she hated
the look in those thick-lashed eyes. It was a warm, almost
loving look, but she didn't feel warm and loving at all.
Not after what he had done to her. Not after what she
had let him do.

Despite the effort it took her, Candace managed to
suppress her disorderly feelings. Civility, she decided,
was in order at present. They were in a public place,
after all, and it wouldn't do for her to create a scene.

"Nick," she said at last, "what are you doing here?"

He glanced down at his shopping cart then back up at
her, his amusement increasing. "Buying groceries."

Caught off guard by his offhand response, she, too,
looked down to study his cart, a frown slowly forming
on her forehead. He should be in New York, racing
around with his fellow rats, not in Dallas. "Why?"

"To eat. It's a bad habit I acquired as a kid—from

infancy, to tell you the truth. And I hate to tell you, but it looks like you've got the same bad habit as well.''

His casual disregard for answering her straightforwardly irritated her. ''No. I mean, why are you here?''

''I told you, to buy groc—''

''Will you stop it? You know what I mean. Why are you in Dallas? You're supposed to be in New York. You left here and went there right after Tony and Elise's wedding.''

''Yeah, and I came back again.''

Candace could see that. ''For a visit?'' Oh, please say that's the reason, Nick. Please say you're only here for a short time, the shorter the better, and that you haven't come back on any kind of permanent or semipermanent basis.

But if he had come back for a visit, who was he visiting? His brother Tony had moved to New York, where his and Nick's family lives, and where Nick should be right now. And as far as Candace knew, he had no other relatives living in town, or even nearby.

Nick stared off into space for a moment, reluctant to answer. ''No, not exactly for a visit.''

Candace got a sinking feeling inside as she realized that he *was* here permanently. He had come back for reasons known only to him, reasons that she strongly suspected might include her.

''I live here now,'' he said.

Her mouth and throat immediately went dry, and when she spoke, there was a noticeable crack in her voice. ''You do?'' Hearing the trepidation, the vulnerability in her tone, she wanted to kick herself. She couldn't afford to show him how susceptible she was to him, how vulnerable he made her feel. Vulnerable, weak in the knees, just at the thought of how they had been together, all warm and loving, that one time in her apartment.

"Yeah," he said, "I moved here a couple of weeks ago. Lock, stock, and fax machines." His grin broadened. "As a matter of fact, we're sort of neighbors."

"Neighbors?" Oh, dear heaven, Candace thought, feeling the sinking feeling in her stomach take a sudden plunge to her toes. The situation was getting worse by the minute. "You've moved into my apartment complex?"

"No. I looked there, but they didn't have a three-bedroom unit available, only a two-bedroom. And with all my stuff, I definitely needed three bedrooms. Of course, four would have been better, but I'm used to cramped quarters."

Three bedrooms? she wondered. What did an unmarried man need with three bedrooms? And then the answer hit her. Probably so he wouldn't have trouble sleeping around, she decided. With that many bedrooms, he could take a different girl into a different bedroom each night and never get their names confused.

"I'm working out of my house," he said.

His casual explanation took some of the venom out of her thoughts. So, he needed the extra room for business purposes, not his amorous pursuits.

"Wait a minute," she said. "A house? You bought a house in my neighborhood?"

"No, I didn't buy it. I'm just leasing it. One of those short-term six-month things that I can get out of in a hurry if I feel the need. It's not like New York, where you move into a place and stay there for years because nothing better's available. If everything goes as well as it has been these last two weeks, I hope to be moving to larger quarters before the end of the year. Maybe sooner. Who knows?"

"You're saying that you'll be moving to another part of Dallas?" And not back to New York where he belonged? Rats, she thought.

"Yeah. This town's got terrific potential. More opportunities than I ever thought. Doors have been opening left and right for me. I've already got a pretty impressive list of accounts. Ten so far."

"That's really amazing," Candace said, hoping she sounded impressed rather than sarcastic.

Nick nodded, pleased with his own achievement. "You can say that again. I thought breaking into the Dallas ad market would be kind of rough. You know, penetrating the good-old-boy network and all that. But everyone I've met has been highly receptive to new ideas. *My* new ideas."

"Congratulations. But back to this business about your house . . ."

"What about it?"

"Just exactly where is it?"

"Oh, across the street and down the block a ways from your place."

Across the street and down the block . . . Candace delved deep into her memory, trying to picture her neighborhood. In her mind's eye she saw her street, a heavily trafficked thoroughfare at almost any hour of the day or night. On one side lay her apartment complex and a city park, complete with golf course, lighted softball diamonds, and a large playground for children. On the other side, houses that had been built back in the thirties and forties, marched for at least a mile or more. Big one- and two-story affairs made of stone and brick, with steeply sloping front lawns and trees that would make a lumberjack envious.

Nick could afford to lease one of those places? Heavens, she thought. The rent alone probably set him back a small fortune each month. His free-lance business *must* be good.

"Oops, we'd better move out of the way," Nick said. "I think we're beginning to block traffic."

He grabbed the end of her cart and pulled on it, offering a smile of apology at the middle-aged woman who passed by them. "Sorry."

"Oh, that's quite all right," the woman said, returning his smile warmly.

Candace suppressed a grimace. Sure, the woman could smile at him. She didn't know what Nick was capable of doing, that he could make an intelligent woman lose all sense of reason and responsibility, much like a powerful hallucinogenic could do. The man should be declared a controlled substance, he was so dangerous.

Nick watched Candace look at the retreating woman's back and felt a rush of exuberance surge through him. He wanted to laugh out loud with joy. By appearing out of the blue as he had, he had caught Candace completely off balance. And that's just how he wanted her. For a while longer, at least. He would wait until the time was just right, and then he would let her turn him into putty in her hands.

"Where to next?" Nick asked, looking over her shoulder to consult her shopping list.

Candace whirled around in confusion, taking a quick backward step when she found his face too close to her own. "What?"

"Frozen foods, or fresh produce? Where do we go?"

"Fresh produce." Secretly, she wished he would vanish into thin air. She didn't want or need him trailing her. She didn't want or need him, period.

"Good. The fresh stuff is much better for you."

Don't lose it, McFarren, Candace told herself as Nick pulled her basket along with his. Just stay cool.

He was being slightly overbearing and predatory, sticking with her this way, but she wasn't going to let his audacious behavior get to her. She might feel an overwhelming need to run as fast and as far away from him as she could, but she was going to repress that urge and just stay calm. She knew it would only make matters worse, only make him more determined, if she let him see how apprehensive he made her.

"You know," Nick said, "history is repeating itself, even as we speak."

History was repeating itself? What kind of come-on gambit was this? "How is it doing that?"

"Tony and Elise met in a supermarket."

Candace snorted dryly. "No, they didn't."

"Yeah, they did. They met in a supermarket, and later that same night she fixed dinner for him. It had to be love, or chemistry, or one of those sudden-attraction type things."

"I might agree with your sudden-attraction theory, but not the supermarket, because they met in the parking lot of their apartment complex the day he moved in. And she didn't fix him dinner; she let him buy dinner for her."

"Mmm, I don't think so."

"Trust me, Nick, I know what I'm talking about. I got it straight from the source."

"Tony?"

"No, Elise."

"Well, my brother tells a slightly different story."

"Then your brother has his facts a little confused. Not that that's a bad thing. It's normal, if you really want to know."

"How's that?"

"It's simple. Most guys don't retain information of a personal nature. I suppose it's not important enough to them. Too trivial, you know? The big stuff, sure, like when a project at work has to be finished or when the monthly mortgage and car payment is due. Even certain phone numbers. But little things that are unimportant to them, that are really more intimate, now that's where we women shine. Our minds are like little steel traps."

Nick grinned. She had brought up the subject of intimacy; he hadn't. But now that she had raised the topic, brought it to the surface, however unintentionally, he wasn't about to let the opportunity to explore it further escape him.

"I hope you're speaking in general terms, not specific ones. Because I'm not like that. I remember the little things, the intimate, trivial stuff, as you called it. It's very important. Very necessary."

Where Nick and intimacy were concerned, Candace didn't doubt him for a moment. Because he came from worldly New York, she had a feeling that the women in his past were professionals, closely connected to his own field. Artists, models, corporate executives . . . More than likely, he had been intimate with quite a number of women in his life. Women of every shape, size, and age. Women from varying backgrounds, sophisticated and glamorous, who had class and breeding. Naturally that didn't include the girls he had dated in high school, the ones who had probably taught him the rudiments of how to romance a member of the opposite sex, make them willing and eager to cooperate. But she didn't include herself in that category. She had been a one-time-only encounter for him, never to be repeated again.

And then a sudden thought struck her. With Nick's

kind of background, his track record where women were concerned, what had he ever seen in her, a lowly secretary? What did she have that appealed to him, to his basic masculine nature? It couldn't have been her looks, because, heaven only knew, she wasn't a raving beauty, to her way of thinking. Her figure wasn't anything to brag about, either. It tended to have more curves than angles, especially when she got depressed and tried to alleviate her moodiness by consuming a whole box of chocolates.

Her personality perhaps?

No, not that either, Candace decided. She knew that if she had to put a label on herself, call herself something that would describe her personality, it would have to be a modern-day wallflower, a homebody, a drudge. She led a very uneventful life. She never dressed up in glamorous clothes, because she didn't have any. She didn't go to a glamorous job, and she didn't meet different and exciting people. No, "different" fit, but she scratched "exciting." The guys in the R & D lab weren't run-of-the-mill by any means. But they could never be called exciting. Just weird.

So what had been the attraction? Of all the women he could have had, why had he singled her out? And more importantly, why had he gone to bed with her?

Face it, she told herself. Nick was in a strange town, surrounded by strangers; he got lonely and horny, and you were the only thing available.

That made about as much sense as anything to Candace.

"Have you got everything?" Nick asked later as they made their way to the checkout registers.

Candace eyed her grocery cart and had to stifle a groan. She had been so immersed in her thoughts, she hadn't paid attention to what she was putting in her basket. But she should have, because she had enough stuff to last her well over a month. Oh, well. Buying it now would save her another trip to the market later on. She just hoped she had enough in her checking account to pay for it all.

"Yeah," she said. "I've got everything."

Much later, as they exited the supermarket, Nick paused for a moment outside the automatic doors. "I guess I'll be seeing you around."

Feeling an emotion that she refused to identify as disappointment, Candace nodded. "Yeah, see ya."

Turning, she pushed her cart slowly toward her car, a frown marring her forehead. He hadn't come on to her, hadn't laid the tired old line of "my place or yours?" on her, either. More surprising, though, was the fact that he hadn't even once brought up the subject of their night together.

Probably because it hadn't meant anything to him, she decided. *She* hadn't meant anything to him. So what if their encounter had disrupted her life for weeks afterward, leaving her wallowing in guilt? It hadn't meant a thing to him. She had been just another warm, feminine body to him, someone to keep him company for a few hours while he—what was the old-fashioned term? Oh yeah. Satisfied his lusts.

The jerk.

It was a good thing he didn't mean anything to her. Because if he did, if she cared about him the least little bit, he could have very easily broken her heart just now. But he was nothing to her. And obviously, she was nothing to him.

Making certain all the bags were packed securely in

the trunk of her car, Candace slammed the lid and climbed behind the wheel.

Okay. If that's how Nick Giulianni wanted to play it, as though nothing had happened between them, as though the one night they had spent in bed together wasn't worth remembering, then fine. The next time they ran into each other, if there was a next time, she would behave just as cool and unaffected as he.

"Hi," Nick said as he cradled the phone's receiver between his chin and shoulder. With both hands free, he could talk and put away groceries at the same time.

"Hi, yourself," Courtney said on the other end of the line.

"Are you busy?"

"I'm always busy, but I can make time for you. What's up?"

"I thought you might want to know that Candy was just where you said she'd be."

"At the supermarket or the dry cleaners?"

"Supermarket."

"Well, this is Saturday. I knew it would have to be one place or the other. She's so predictable. Where'd you find her?"

"In the packaged snack section, loading up on potato chips and cookies."

"Uh-oh," Courtney said. "This isn't a good sign."

"Why? What's wrong?"

"It sounds like she's depressed. She always pigs out on junk food when she gets depressed." And with Don being out of town, missing her birthday, Courtney thought, Candace's depression was very understandable.

"How about fresh produce?"

"Fresh produce?" Courtney's assumption took a sudden reverse. "Did she buy much?"

"Yeah, just about one of everything," Nick said. "Even something called a jicama. Whatever that is."

"Mmm! Maybe she's not as depressed as I'd thought. Maybe she's just confused."

"Oh, she's that, all right. You should have seen her face this morning when she saw me pop up from out of nowhere."

"You didn't say anything to her, did you?"

"I said hello."

"No, I mean about the other. About why you were there. That I told you."

"No. I just told her I was buying groceries. Which I really was. A man's gotta eat, you know, even when he is in the middle of stalking an elusive wild female of the Homo sapiens species."

"Candy's not wild, Nick."

"Tell me about it. But you can't deny that she is elusive."

Courtney laughed. "Not for much longer. If we play our cards right, you'll have her bagged and mounted before you know it. Before *she* knows it."

"Whoa! Wait just a minute, Court."

"I'm sorry. Scratch the 'mounted' part."

"No, that's okay. 'Mounted,' I can handle." With more eagerness than you can imagine, my friend, he thought. "It was the 'bagged' part I object to. I don't want to cage or shackle her. I like her just the way she is."

"I know. The job we have in store for us is to get her to return that sentiment. Which, I imagine, she does already, to a degree. We've just got to loosen her up a little, make her see reality for the way it really is."

"Yeah," Nick said. "So, what's next on our agenda?

Where do I waylay her next?"

"Waylay?"

"Yeah, you know, ambush, trap, strike."

Courtney cleared her throat. "Nick, have you been watching a lot of old westerns on TV or something since you moved down here?"

"No, I haven't had time. Why? Did I say something wrong? I thought that's how all you Texans talked."

"We might have, a hundred or so years ago, but we don't today. Now we use terms like game plan, strategy, tactics—stuff like that."

"Don't tell me, let me guess. Is networking included in this new vocabulary of yours?"

"Of course. That's what we're doing right now—networking."

Nick stifled a groan. Was there no getting away from trendy Yuppie-isms? Obviously not, he decided. "So, what's up next, coach?"

"I thought a little dinner party would be in order right about now."

"How little is little?"

"Oh, ten or fifteen people. No, make that sixteen. Odd numbers always make me nervous."

"This little dinner party is going to be at your place, I hope. Mine won't hold that many people."

"Of course I'll have it at my place. I'm the hostess."

"Any special occasion? Or are you doing this just for my benefit?"

"A little of both, as a matter of fact. You see, I think it's about time you got some public exposure, and what better way of getting it than to introduce you to some fairly influential associates of mine. Who knows? We might even manage to swing a little business your way."

Nick hesitated a moment, uncertain if he should thank

Courtney for being so considerate, or scold her for taking too much for granted. He had already made a pretty good start in getting his name, his company, his talent, before the Dallas public eye. All he needed was a little more time, a few more accounts, and he would have established himself.

"Court, honey," he said, "I appreciate what you're trying to do. I really do. But please, don't go to all this trouble on my account."

"Having business associates and a few friends over for dinner is no trouble at all, Nick. It's a pleasure. And to be perfectly honest, it's somewhat overdue. The fact is, if I ignore these associates and friends for much longer, they're going to start scratching me off their lists. And I can't have that. For the most part, they all have hefty bank balances, and at one time or another they've all needed a good lawyer. So entertaining them in the privacy of my home is just naturally good for business. But I would have thought that coming from the land of the power breakfast and the business lunch and dinner, you would already know that."

"That's just it, Court. I've never fed a client dinner in my home. I always took them to a restaurant."

"Four-star, I'll bet."

"Sometimes."

"Well, I guess that's the difference between New York and Dallas," Courtney said. "We tend to be a little more casual and a little more personal down here. We like inviting people into our homes and treating them like family instead of ordinary business associates. When we do that, they tend to remember us. Trust me. I know what I'm talking about."

"Are you saying that I need to invite my handful of clients over here to my house for a backyard barbecue?"

"No, not at all. I'm just saying you might want to consider the possibility—once you're really settled in, of course. You want to impress them, make them feel special. You certainly don't want them to feel sorry for you. And living out of unpacked boxes, as I'm sure you still are, is definitely a sign you're begging for their pity."

"Uh-huh. I'll take your suggestion under advisement."

"You do that. And when the time finally comes for you to entertain, make sure you've got a hostess at the front door to smile and greet your guests."

"By 'hostess,' I assume you're referring to—"

"Candy. Who else?"

"Well, at the rate I'm going with her, I don't suppose I'll have to worry about buying paper plates and whipping up a special barbecue sauce until the beginning of the next century."

"Surely not that long," Courtney said.

"Weren't you the one who told me to take it slow and easy at first with her?"

"Yes, but I didn't mean for you to crawl at a snail's pace. Just give her some time, let her get used to the fact that you're in town again, and that you're not back up in the jungles of Manhattan. She needs to see you in a few of her old haunts and know that you're not going to pounce on her like you did the first night you two were alone. Which, if you don't mind my saying so, was a big mistake."

A pain registered in the middle of Nick's chest, causing him to hesitate a moment. "Is that what she told you?"

"No, that's my own estimation of the situation."

"Well, you're wrong. It wasn't a mistake. We did the right thing."

"Stop getting so defensive, Nick. I'm not blaming you. And I'm certainly not blaming Candy. I know you both wanted it to happen. Candy more than you, probably, even though getting her to admit it would be like pulling teeth. It's just that, under the circumstances, it might have been better if you two had waited a little bit, gotten to know each other first."

I know all I need to know, Nick thought.

He loved Candace and would do whatever it took to get her to return that love to him. But explaining that to Courtney wouldn't be easy, so he wasn't going to try. The lady might have been a terrific friend to him since he'd first met her, but it hadn't taken him long to realize that she thought only in terms of black and white, right and wrong. To Ms. Courtney Ames, there was no in-between.

"That's what I'm trying to do now," Nick said. "I want Candy to get to know me, not be afraid of me."

"And with my help, she won't be. Give her time, she'll come around to our way of thinking. Wait and see."

5

"A DINNER PARTY?" CANDACE asked, surprised. "At your place?" She had always dropped by Courtney's whenever she felt like it. But to get a verbal invitation like this, out of the clear blue? She felt honored, and at the same time a little intimidated.

"Will you come?" Courtney asked.

"Gosh, Court, I don't know. What's going on?"

"Nothing important, really. It's just an intimate little gathering for a few friends. You are one of my friends, you know."

"Yes, but you've never invited me to one of these things before."

"That's because I've only given one other, and you couldn't come because you were out of town at the time."

"I was?"

"Yes. Don't you remember?"

Candace frowned, trying to recall the time and failing miserably. "No."

"Come on. It was just a couple of years ago; surely

61

you can remember that far back. You had to rush out to New Mexico to see your dad. He'd gotten sick or something. You were gone for well over a week.''

"Oh, yeah! Now I remember. But Daddy wasn't sick. Not really. He had just broken his leg.''

"Was that all it was? A broken leg? I thought he'd had major surgery or something. Jeez, the way you flew out of town, I got the impression it was a life-and-death situation.''

The way her father had carried on when he had phoned her, he'd made it sound life-and-death, too, Candace reflected. "No, just a broken leg.''

"Wait a minute. Where was his wife? Why didn't she take care of him?''

"Well, they were sort of separated at the time." Just one of the many times her father and Berniece, his wife, had let a petty lovers' quarrel get so far out of hand that Berniece's only option was to walk out and let the situation cool down, Candace thought.

"So," Courtney said, "he made you fly all the way out there from Dallas just to hold his hand.''

"Yeah, but I didn't mind.''

That was the problem with Candace, Courtney decided. She would drop whatever she was doing and put her own life on hold interminably just to please her parents. Even as far back as kindergarten, Candace's parents had always come first with her. Whatever they wanted of her, she gave them, did for them. Even to this day, she was the perfect daughter, the ideal "good little girl.'' Too bad she had never taken time to please herself.

Courtney heaved a sigh. "I know you didn't mind. I wasn't suggesting that you did. But let's get back to the subject of dinner. Will you be able to come?''

"Sure, I guess so.''

"Good. Remember now, it's Saturday, the day after tomorrow, at eight at my place. And wear something casually elegant."

"In other words, no jeans, is that it?"

"You got it."

"How about a guest? Can I bring one?"

Courtney issued a silent moan, knowing to whom Candace was referring, even though she hadn't mentioned him by name. But Candace didn't need to. Courtney knew she meant Don and not Nick. "Well, no offense, but I'd rather you wouldn't. Not that I wouldn't mind another guest, it's just that I've already got the seating arrangements made out, and it's perfect. You know, boy, girl, boy, girl. That sort of thing. I really have no more room for the odd male at my table." The moment the words left her lips, she wished she could retract them. "Not that I'm suggesting Don is odd or anything."

Candace laughed. "I know what you meant."

"I thought you might." *Prayed* she might was more like it, Courtney thought. At this point, so early in the game, she couldn't afford to risk putting Candace on the defensive; she might be so offended that she would alienate herself altogether. And an alienated Candace was the last thing Courtney wanted. She had to keep the lines of communication open between them, because Nick needed all the help he could get, and she was going to give him her very best, come hell or high water.

"The only reason I asked," Candace said, "is because Don might be in town this weekend."

"Might be?"

"Um-hmm."

"You're not sure?"

"No."

What a major pain-in-the-neck jerk, Courtney mused.

Did the guy ever call Candace in advance these days? Or did he just phone her at the last minute when he was in town and had nothing better to do, and no one better to do it with?

"When did you last hear from him?" Courtney asked.

"Last Sunday night," Candace said.

"He'd been gone all week long, hadn't he?" Of course he had, Courtney thought. He missed your birthday, and considerate moron that he is, he didn't even send you so much as a present or a card.

"Yes."

"So how long did you get to spend with him?"

"Well, we weren't actually together. We talked on the phone for a while. Ten minutes or so, I guess."

Ten minutes, Courtney thought. What a sacrifice. "And did he make a date with you for this weekend?"

"Not exactly. He did say something about catching me later, the next time he came through town, but his flight to Des Moines was called and he had to leave before we could make any definite plans."

A ten-minute layover phone call? Courtney fumed in silence. That was all Candace meant to Don these days— a brief phone call between flights? When would Candace ever learn the guy didn't care as much for her as she cared for him? Probably never, she decided, hearing a beep in her ear that told her a call was coming through on her call-waiting line.

"Darn it," Courtney said, "I'm going to have to let you go. I'm getting another call, and I've got a hunch it's David."

"David Ballard? That tall, sexy lawyer you work with?"

"Work *for,* not with," Courtney said. "Remember, he's a senior partner while technically I'm just a junior."

"I don't care what you are. I still think he's a hunk."

"You're not the only one. All the girls in the office think so, too. In fact, he's probably the only lawyer in town who gets fan mail. But enough about him. Don't forget about this coming Saturday night. Seven o'clock sharp. Can I count on you to be there?"

"Yeah, sure."

"Good."

Her phone call with Courtney ended, Candace padded barefoot into her bedroom to peruse her wardrobe. "Casually elegant," Courtney had said. To Candace, that translated into something pretty and attractive but primarily comfortable. Not the suits, dresses, or skirts, sweaters, and blouses that she usually wore to work. And definitely not jeans or sweats, either.

But the more Candace looked at her current clothes, pushing one hanger after another aside, the more depressed she became. She didn't own anything that closely resembled elegant. Basic and durable, yes, but elegant? No way.

"Face it, McFarren," she muttered to herself. "You're going to have to bite the bullet and go shopping."

She turned to the mirror atop her dresser, caught a glimpse of her reflection, and smiled. "Yippeee!"

Courtney stood in the doorway of her elegantly trendy suburban home, smiling at her late-arriving guests. As they neared the raised front entry she chanced a peek at the street, looking for another set of headlights that might belong to Candace. Where the devil was that girl? Courtney hoped she hadn't had car trouble or, God forbid, an accident.

"I'm so glad you could make it!" Courtney said,

welcoming the newcomers, a fellow attorney and his
wife. What was the woman's name? She couldn't remember clearly. She knew his was Jim, but was the
wife's Janet, Jeannie, or Joan?

"I wouldn't have missed coming tonight for the
world," the woman said. "I had to call all over town
for a baby-sitter and finally found one at the last minute."

"She's trustworthy, I hope," Courtney said, starting
to close her front door behind them. Just at that moment,
though, she spotted a pair of headlights stopping near
the foot of her circular drive. Candace, she thought.
Well, better to be late than not show up at all. She had
worked too hard setting up this evening.

"He," the husband said, interrupting Courtney's
thoughts. "The baby-sitter is a he, not a she. And he
looks like a throwback to the late sixties. Weird hair,
rock T-shirt, and torn jeans. A died-in-the-wool hippy
reject if I ever saw one."

"That's punk, dear," the wife said. "Today it's punk,
or headbanger, not hippy."

"Whatever," the man said. "I just hope the kids are
still in one piece when we get home."

The wife turned to give Courtney a dry look. "The
question is, will the sitter still be in one piece? Our kids
have the dubious honor of being the terrors of the neighborhood."

"Well, both of you can forget about them for a while,"
Courtney said. "In fact, just forget about everything
except having a good time. I've got a table full of goodies
in the kitchen, and if you'd like a drink, Jim, fix what
you'd like. Dinner's not going to be until eight or so."

"Who's tending bar?" the husband asked.

"It's going to be self-serve tonight, I'm afraid,"
Courtney said. "But you'll find all the makings you'll

need behind the wet bar in the game room. You know where it is, don't you, Jim? Down the stairs and to the right.''

"You bet," he said. "You've still got your pool table, haven't you?"

"Of course," Courtney said. She would never dream of parting with her pool table; it had been the last thing her father had ever given to her. And added to its highly sentimental value was the fact that it had been the main reason she had decided to invest in a house, rather than continuing to live in her old apartment—she had needed a place to put it. Too bad she didn't play, she thought. One day she would have to learn how.

"Good," Jim said. "I've been looking forward all week long to tonight. I intend to get even with Dave for beating the socks off me the last time we played.''

"Not too even, I hope," his wife said. "No betting tonight, remember? Not on any ball games that might be on TV or on pool.''

Jim held up his right hand. "I solemnly swear that my loose change will never leave my pockets.''

"It had better not.''

At that moment Candace slowly emerged into the halo of light that spilled away from the front entrance. Courtney, still standing at the opened door, turned and saw her, her eyes widening at the sight of her old friend. Candace, she realized, had not only taken pains with her hair, she had been shopping as well.

"Well, look at you," Courtney said, smiling. "Aren't you spiffy this evening?''

Self-consciously, Candace ran a hand down one slender black-panted leg as the other tugged at the modestly dipping neckline of her pale pink silk Charmeuse blouse. "I'm not overdressed, am I? I know you said that tonight was going to be casually elegant, but I wasn't sure what that meant exactly.''

"You got it right on target, kiddo," Courtney said. Casually elegant didn't begin to describe the way Candace looked. Drop-dead gorgeous did.

"Am I very late?" Candace asked.

"Well, dinner hasn't been served yet, if that's what you're asking. Come on in. Everybody else is already here."

"Oh, no. I'm the last to arrive?"

"It's all right, Candy. Relax. Loosen up a little and have a good time. Would you like something to drink?"

"Iced tea would be nice, if you have some already made."

"Iced tea? You don't want something with a little more kick to it?"

"I'd better not," Candace said. "I have to drive home tonight, remember?"

Courtney stifled a groan. "All right, since alcohol is out, how about some designer-label water with a twist of lime? That should keep you sober."

"Water sounds fine," Candace said. "But no lime."

"Fine, no lime. You go on into the kitchen and visit with the girls, and I'll get your drink."

Down a flight of stairs and along a short hallway lay Courtney's gourmet kitchen. Candace, who had visited many times before, went inside to join the other women while Courtney journeyed a little farther, on to the back of the house and the game room, where all the men had elected to go.

Once alone, Courtney gave her head an amused shake. Why she ever bothered to plan dinners like this with such care to detail, she never knew. The inevitable always happened; the men would go in one room, while the women stayed in another, the two never sharing their conversations, even though both were usually about the same topics.

"How's it going, guys?" she asked, slipping behind the wet bar to make Candace's drink.

"Great!" a couple of men answered.

"It looks like Janna and I got here at just the right time," Jim said. "Dave's about to slaughter Frank."

Pouring water over ice in a tall glass, Courtney took a moment to watch her boss, David Ballard, in action. Dressed in casual slacks and shirt instead of his usual three-piece suit, he looked lean and trim, less daunting, as he walked around the pool table, eyeing the arrangement of balls on the green felt top. He stopped, carefully lined up a shot, leaning over as he positioned his cue stick, then with a quick jab, he sank two balls in opposite corner pockets at once.

"Yeah," said another, "If he ever gets tired of practicing law, he can always take up pool hustling as a profession."

"Slaughter, huh?" Courtney asked. "Well, just remember to keep it clean, would you, guys? No blood on the floors or walls, and no fighting inside the premises."

Leaving the men to their own primeval devices, that of man trying to get the best of his fellow man, Courtney walked back up the hall to the kitchen. There, she discovered the topic of conversation to be that of men and their shortcomings.

"He's always leaving his socks on the floor where the puppy can run off with them, and then he wonders why he never has a pair that matches," said Janna.

"Better his socks than his underwear," said Roberta.

"Underwear?" Courtney asked, surprised. The idea of Roberta's husband, Sherman, prancing around his house in the buff made her stifle a giggle. The couple's three children were grown and out on their own, and he and Roberta had the house all to themselves, so it wasn't the idea of his nudity fetish that amused Courtney as much as it was the notion of Sherman, all two-hundred and sixty pounds of him, letting it all hang out, so to speak.

"He says that wearing his shorts for ten hours makes him break out in a rash," Roberta said with a snort of dry disbelief.

"Maybe they do," Candace said. "I read an article the other day that said some people can become highly allergic to synthetic fibers."

"That's just it," Roberta said. "He doesn't wear synthetic underwear—when he wears them, that is. I buy him nothing but one-hundred-percent cotton."

"Maybe he needs to go see an allergist," Janna suggested.

Roberta gave her a dead-pan look. "My husband go see a doctor when he's not running a hundred and three degrees of fever and throwing up all over the place? Are you kidding? The man's afraid of doctors."

"Roberta, Sherman *is* a doctor," Courtney said.

"That's why he's afraid of them," Roberta said. "He knows what they're capable of doing."

"You really should talk to him about it, though," Janna said.

"Thank you, but no, thank you. I've talked to him so much over the last thirty-one years of our marriage, trying to get him to do things, that I've simply given up. I let him do things his way."

"Thirty-one years?" Janna asked. "Good heavens! Jim and I have only been married for eleven, but sometimes it feels more like fifty. What's your secret? How do you stay married to a man for that length of time and not go crazy or feel like murdering him?''

"It's simple, really," Roberta said, grinning. "You stop listening to him when you don't like hearing what he's saying."

"Just turn a deaf ear," said Leigh, another of Courtney's guests whose age equaled that of Roberta's. "Let him have his say. Let him ramble on for as long as his wind holds out. Just nod, like you're in total agreement with him, even when you're not. Then when he shuts up or falls asleep, you do it your way."

"And that works?" Janna asked, laughing.

"Almost always," Roberta said.

"You and I should be taking notes, Candy," Courtney said, just as her oven timer rang.

"Oh, are one of you planning to get married soon?" Leigh asked.

"I'm not," Courtney said, "but it never hurts to be prepared." She slipped an oven mitt on her hand and opened the oven door, letting the fragrant aroma of freshly baked bread waft about the kitchen.

"How about you?" Leigh asked, turning to Candace.

"No, I'm not either." But deep in one tiny part of her heart, Candace wished that she were getting married. Having a man around the house, putting up with his bad habits, sounded a lot better than living alone.

"Dinner is ready," Courtney said, slipping the hot bread into a napkin-lined basket then turning around to lower the temperature on her oven.

"I'll go tell Sherman and the others," Roberta said, sliding off her kitchen stool.

"Can we help you carry in anything?" Janna offered.

"No, thank you. You and Leigh just go on into the dining room. I'll be up in a minute."

As the others filed out, climbing the short flight of stairs to the dining-room–living-room level of the house, Candace stayed behind. ''What do you need me to do?''

''Nothing. I've taken care of everything.'' And are you going to be surprised when you find out what everything is, she thought. ''Oh, if you wouldn't mind—we might need some extra ice and water. You'll find a carafe already filled in the fridge and an ice bucket in the freezer.''

''Sure,'' Candace said.

By the time Candace made it into the dining room, her hands filled with ice bucket and icy-cold water carafe, everyone had found their place at Courtney's long table. As before, when she had visited her friend's lovely new home, Candace found herself envying the elegant rooms, wishing they were her own. Tonight Courtney had outdone herself. China and crystal glistened in the muted light from the chandelier. On the polished mahogany buffet table against the wall, a wide arrangement of vegetables rested in heated chafing dishes. And at the end, standing three layers high on a crystal cake pedestal that Candace knew Courtney had inherited from her maternal grandmother, was a sinful-looking chocolate cake.

And then Candace saw Nick, sitting beside an empty place at the table—her place—and she almost dropped the water carafe.

6

WHAT SHOULD HAVE BEEN A PLEAS-
ant dinner turned into a horrendous ordeal for Candace.
She couldn't enjoy Courtney's well-cooked meal because
she was too conscious of every move that Nick Giulianni
made. At any moment she half expected him to rub his
leg deliberately against hers or to slip his hand below
the table and paw her thigh. But he did neither. He merely
sat beside her and ate, holding up his end of the conversation with the others. It drove her crazy.

Why on earth, she wondered, had Courtney invited
him tonight? He had nothing in common with the others.
They were all lawyers and doctors and their wives, who
had lived in the Dallas area most of their lives. They
weren't single, handsome ad men from New York City.

Thinking on the matter further, Candace realized that
she had nothing in common with the others, either, but
that was beside the point. She was Courtney's friend.
Or, rather, she was supposed to be Courtney's friend.
But after tonight, after having to sit so closely to Nick,

getting whiff after whiff of his intoxicating after-shave lotion and listening to him converse and laugh with the others as though he had known them for ages, she had to wonder. The first chance she got, she would ask Courtney what her motive had been for inviting both of them.

Surely Courtney hadn't asked her to come tonight just so she could watch Nick taunt her, make her feel more guilty than she already did. No, of course she hadn't. Candace knew that Courtney wasn't the vindictive type. Nor was she deviously manipulative, either.

Then why had she so deviously manipulated her into coming here tonight?

Candace's questions grew more and more complex and confusing.

Finally, her long ordeal came to an end—dinner was over. Courtney refused any and all offers of assistance from the women as she cleared the dishes, merely setting them on the buffet.

"I can get these later," she said. "Why don't we all go into the living room and have our coffee and cake in there."

"Now?" Leigh asked.

"Sure, why not?" Courtney said.

"Well, it certainly looks yummy enough," Roberta said, eyeing the towering confection at the end of the buffet, "but I couldn't eat another bite at the moment."

"I couldn't, either," Janna echoed.

The only thing that appeals to me right now, Candace thought, casting a sidelong glance at Courtney, is your head next to Nick's on a silver platter. What the devil are you up to, friend?

"You really outdid yourself on the steaks, Courtney," Nick said, pushing himself away from the table. "I've always heard how great Texas beef was, and now I know what all the raving was about. You cooked mine just right.''

"Thank you," Courtney said with a smile. "But I can't take all the credit. Neither can the state of Texas, for that matter. You see, they're from Nebraska, by way of Chicago.''

"No kidding?" Nick asked.

"Nope, no kidding."

"Hmm. Another myth shot down in flames," he said.

As he moved away from the table Candace noticed that he walked a bit strangely, a little on the cocky and arrogant side. She frowned. He had sat beside her for a half hour, but that couldn't have affected his mobility, could it?

And then she glanced down and saw the cause of his odd gait. Cowboy boots. Shiny black cowboy boots with pointed toes and two-inch-high heels.

Good Lord, she thought, feeling laughter well up in her throat. He was trying to go native. Well, he would never make it. An Italian cowboy? Who had ever heard of such a thing?

"Well, since no one is interested in having cake right away," Courtney said, interrupting Candace's musings, "I suppose we'll just save it for later. Can I interest anyone in a brandy or a liqueur?"

"Why don't we save that for later, too?" David suggested, leaning close to Courtney as he brushed past her. "Give us a chance to digest what we've already eaten. If you don't, you'll have to roll us all out of here in wheelbarrows."

In the living room, Courtney had turned the lamps down to a muted glow, giving the entire room a feeling of total comfort. With a delicious dinner behind them, more pleasant conversation and a mouth-watering dessert awaiting them, everyone fell into a genial mood.

Everyone, that is, except Candace. She made certain that she sat nowhere near Nick. When he settled himself on Courtney's long sofa, she slipped into one of the high wingback chairs at the far end of the room. She even made sure that there were others between them so she wouldn't have to look at him.

The conversation began again. As David Ballard told a humorous courtroom anecdote that he had personally experienced, Candace's mind began to wander back to the questions that had plagued her throughout dinner. Why *had* Courtney invited her tonight? Obviously, she had known that Nick was coming; she had invited him, so his presence was hardly a coincidence. And Courtney knew full well of the self-torment that Candace had endured because of her one-time-only fling with Nick. So, why had she—

Suddenly such a horrible thought struck Candace that it made her stomach churn. No, she thought, not that. Surely, that hadn't been the reason.

She looked across the room and studied Courtney, who sat with her long legs curled beneath her in a chair, looking every inch the contented sophisticated hostess. Her attention, Candace saw, was totally on Nick. Leaning forward slightly, giving the impression of shifting her position, she got a clear view of Nick and his face. He gazed straight at Courtney, and the look Candace saw in his eye could only be described as conspiratorial.

Oh, no, not Courtney, too, she thought. Nick wasn't her type. Courtney wasn't Nick's type, either.

But they *had* spent some time together, she told herself. A lot of time, as a matter of fact. They had met before Tony and Elise's wedding, during it, and afterward she had driven him to the airport. Good Lord, perhaps she wasn't the only woman Nick had made love to when he had been in Dallas two months ago. Perhaps he had made love to Courtney as well. And if that were the case, then Nick had used her. As he was now using Courtney?

"You're certainly being quiet this evening—Candy, isn't it?"

Candace blinked, her increasingly nauseating train of thought interrupted. She turned and looked at David, who had spoken to her.

"I guess I've been too busy listening to what everybody else has had to say."

David nodded, a grin appearing at the corners of his well-shaped mouth. "We're hogging the conversation, is that what you're saying?"

"No, not at all!"

"Come on, you don't have to be polite. We're lawyers; we're used to hogging the floor. Of course, you understand that being effusive talkers is the nature of our profession."

"You weren't hogging anything, honest. It's just that I haven't had anything interesting to contribute."

"I find that hard to believe—it is Candy, isn't it?"

"Yes."

"A bright-looking young woman like you should have plenty to contribute."

Bright looking? The compliment pleased Candace more than she cared to admit. Normally, men commented on her blond, blue-eyed, somewhat healthy Nordic appearance first, rather than on her intelligence. Big boobs and an empty brain; that's what most men seemed to prefer. But obviously not David Ballard. He didn't seem to be like most men. He certainly wasn't like Nick Giulianni.

"When I feel the need, I'll say something," she said, feeling calm overtake her disquietude. For the first time since she had spied Nick in the dining room, she began to relax.

"You have no opinions on the oil crisis or the state-tax situation?"

"Lots," she said without reservation.

"Like what, for instance?" David asked.

"Well, as for oil, we use much too much of it, and we don't conserve nearly enough. We need to find alternative sources of energy. And as for the state tax—we wouldn't need to raise taxes at all if we could only get the legislators down in Austin to implement a lottery system."

"You approve of gambling?"

Candace shrugged. "No more or no less than the next person. I'm not an addict, so the notion of gambling doesn't really bother me. If I don't want to buy a lottery ticket, or I don't have the money to buy one, then I won't. But it would be nice to come into some unexpected money occasionally. And I'm sure the state treasurer would appreciate the added income, too. If nothing else, it would keep him off our backs—or, rather, out of our bank accounts—for a while."

David studied her a moment with his inquisitive, somewhat judgmental hazel eyes. "Interesting," he said at last.

"What is?"

"Your views on politics."

Candace laughed. "They're no different from anyone else's."

"Don't be too sure about that. There are a lot of folks in this state who don't hold with the idea of games of chance of any sort."

"I know, but we did vote in horse racing, didn't we? What's the technical name for it, pari-mutuel betting?"

"That's it, all right."

"Well, there you are. If we can get that past all the old stick-in-the-muds in this state, then we can vote in just about anything else we want. If we really put our minds to it. Look what we did for bingo. Of course, we have to get it past the elected legislators. Sometimes they're the worst of all."

"What's the matter, don't you trust politicians?"

"Some of them I do, but most of them I don't."

"Why not?"

"Because most of them are in office mainly for what they can get out of it for themselves, not for the voters who elected them in the first place. But every once in a while someone will come along who's honest and sincere. He does his dead-level best to keep the promises he made to his constituents back home. Her constituents too. I wouldn't want to be thought of as a sexist about this. Or anything else, for that matter."

"Never," David said. "At least you won't hear me call you that."

"Call her what?" Courtney asked, having caught the very end of his remark.

"A sexist," David said. "I told Candy I'd never call her a sexist."

"She can't be," Roberta said. "Only men are that."

"Women can be sexist, too," her husband said.

"No, Sherman, women are feminists," Janna said.

"Women can be both sexists and feminists," Leigh said. "Men can't be, though." She cast her husband a sly sidelong glance. "They're either feminists or chauvinists. There is no in-between."

"Now, wait a minute," her husband said, choosing

that moment to leap into the conversation. "Are you saying I'm a chauvinist?"

"Well, you're certainly not a feminist, dear. By any stretch of the imagination."

"Hey, I help you do dishes, don't I?"

"Yes."

"And as I recall, I changed my fair share of diapers when the kids were little."

"Only the wet ones," Leigh said. "You left the really messy ones for me to tackle. But that's all right, I still love you. Queasy stomach and all."

"Speaking of diapers . . ." At Courtney's unfinished comment, all conversation ceased. Every head in the room turned in her direction. Seeing the expectant expressions on their faces, she laughed. "No, no, no, not me. Lindsey Vining. She works in our office. She's the one who's pregnant. She just made the announcement the other day that she's due in about six and a half months."

"Lindsey's . . . ?" David's brows lifted in surprise as his hand made an arcing motion in front of his stomach.

"Yes, Lindsey," Courtney said.

"I didn't even know she was married."

"You didn't know? Where have you been, David? She got married two years ago. Remember the ten dollars you chipped in to help buy her a wedding present?"

"No. But then why should I remember it? It seems I'm always chipping in ten dollars, for one person, one cause or another around that office. I'm amazed we manage to get any work done."

"Well, trust me, Lindsey's married," Courtney said.

"And she's due when?"

"In six and a half months."

"Did she say anything about coming back to work after the baby was born?"

"No," Courtney said. "But she really didn't need to say it. I got the feeling that she's going to stay home, become a full-time wife and mommy."

David sighed. "Damn. Then I guess we'd better start putting out feelers first thing Monday morning to find a replacement for her. It's going to take us at least six months just to train somebody. Lindsey's the best office manager we've had in years."

"Surely not that long," Candace said, thinking of the hundreds of experienced secretaries in Dallas who would jump at the chance to work for David and Courtney's highly prestigious law firm.

"You'd be surprised," David said. "All the good office managers, the ones with really level heads on their shoulders and the ability to do the job, are already taken."

Courtney straightened sharply, her eyes widening as she looked at Candace. "I know of one who isn't."

David, seeing the direction of her gaze, turned and looked at Candace as well. "Yeah, me too."

Candace sat still for a moment, looking first at Courtney and then David, their unspoken thoughts taking but a moment to sink in. She shook her head briskly. "No, not me. Forget it, you two."

"But you'd be perfect for the job," Courtney said.

"Oh, come on. I'm not an office manager. I'm just a secretary."

"You're a lot more than *just* a secretary, and you know it," Courtney said. "You run that office—the whole R and D division, for that matter."

"No, I don't. Dr. Franklin does. He's in charge."

"In charge of his space-cadet scientists maybe,"

Courtney said. "But without you, his department would be in a shambles. Take some credit once in a while, Candy. You're invaluable to that man."

"Well, maybe I am, and maybe I'm not," Candace said. "That really isn't the issue."

"Then what is the issue?" David asked.

"For one thing, I've never been an office manager before. At least, not officially. I wouldn't know the first thing to do."

"You could learn. And a bright lady like you wouldn't take six months to get the hang of the job, either. You'd get the knack of it right away."

Candace thought about it a moment, tempted by the offer. She had been to Courtney's office more than once and had all but drooled over the lawyers' plush facilities. Even the reception area of the firm was lavish, complete with potted plants, leather chairs, original works of art on the walls, and a deep-pile carpet underfoot. The small, almost stark cubicle where she slaved day after day paled in comparison. Not only did Courtney's surroundings appeal to Candace, but the notion of a higher salary, commensurate with what she was worth, sounded very nice. No more icky smells coming out of the lab down the hall, either. No more wearing white lab coats over her clothes. No more walking a half a mile across a parking lot to her building. Candace was tempted.

"No, I'm sorry," she said. "Thank you, but I can't accept it."

"Why not?" David asked. "If it's the money that's holding you back, we'd be more than willing to negotiate, I assure you."

"No, it's not about money. I know without asking that you could pay me more than what I'm getting now."

"Then what's the problem?" he asked.

"Well, to put it frankly, it's Court."

"Me?" Courtney asked.

"And me too," Candace said. "We're best friends, for heaven's sake. Can you imagine the two of us under the same roof together, eight to ten hours a day? We never would get any work done. We'd be talking to each other, planning lunch and shopping trips. You'd lose all of your clients, and I'd end up getting fired."

David chuckled, nodding. "I hadn't considered that angle."

"Neither had I," Courtney said.

"I hate to interrupt," Sherman said. "But the mention of offers has me wondering."

"About what?" Courtney asked.

"About the offer of coffee and cake you made earlier. Does it still hold?"

"My gracious, Sherman, you can't be hungry already," his wife said. "After that huge dinner you just put away?"

Sheepishly, Sherman hung his balding head. "What can I say? My sweet tooth wants to eat, too."

"Coffee and cake for ten, coming right up," Courtney said, hopping to her feet.

"Do you need some help," Leigh said, starting to push herself out of her chair.

"No, keep your seat," Candace said. "I'll help. I need the exercise."

"So do I," Leigh said, "but since you're younger and prettier, I'll let you do it."

In the privacy of Courtney's kitchen, Candace helped her arrange a serving tray with cups and saucers and spoons and forks.

"I want to thank you for asking me to work for you," Candace said. "David too. I shouldn't forget to mention him. It was awfully considerate.''

''You're welcome, but there's really no need to thank us, Candy. We were asking you more for our benefit than yours. I know that may sound selfish, but we're in something of a bind. Or rather, we will be in a bind as soon as Lindsey quits to have her baby. You wouldn't believe how absolutely essential a good office manager is in our line of work. They're the quarterback that holds our team together, our den mother, our—''

''I think I get the picture,'' Candace said, laughing.

''Then maybe you should rethink your answer. Take some time to mull it over before you really decide. You know, you're really very good at what you do. You're organized, efficient, always on time . . . In other words, you're everything that we lawyers aren't—that we lawyers don't have time to be. We've got so much on our minds, what with all our clients and caseloads and court dates, the office itself often comes in a dead last on our list of priorities.''

''I can't rethink it, Court. You know yourself that it wouldn't work.''

''I don't know any such thing.''

''The two of us in an office together? No way.''

''All right, so we're friends. So we talk a lot when we're together. Big deal. We can try to curb our normal tendencies, can't we?''

Candace hung her head, her palms sweating at the thought of bringing up the next subject. ''It's not just that.''

''Then what is it?''

''It's Nick.''

''Nick?'' A thoroughly confused look flashed across Courtney's face. ''Nick Giulianni?''

Candace nodded.

"What's he got to do with this? I asked you to work for us, not him."

"Think about it, Court. We've been best friends since kindergarten. You, me, and Ellie. If we'd been boys, we'd have been called the Three Musketeers."

Or the Three Stooges, Courtney thought.

"We've shared everything, even itchy old chicken pox. And while sharing an office does have its appeal, sharing a guy we've both known int—" Candace broke off. "Well, you know what I'm getting at. And I just can't let that come between us. I won't."

"Sharing a guy? The guy being Nick, right?"

"Right."

"Us?"

"Yes." Candace busied herself by getting a carton of cream out of the refrigerator and pouring it into Courtney's cream pitcher.

"I'm not sharing Nick with you. I'm not sharing anybody with anybody. He's just a friend, that's all."

Candace smiled as she lifted the tray and started out of the kitchen. "It's all right, Court. I understand. Really, I do."

A silver cake server in one hand, a filled crystal brandy decanter in the other, Courtney stared stupidly at the empty doorway. "Understand what, for heaven's sake?"

Then suddenly it registered.

"Dear God!"

As the absurdity of Candace's illogical and wildly off-the-wall assumption took deeper root, Courtney couldn't keep from chuckling. Candace honestly thought that she and Nick—

"Lovers? Nick and I? Ridiculous. Absolutely and utterly ridiculous."

Nick loved Candace, not her, and Courtney knew it.

Shaking her head, she started out of the kitchen, intending to put the previous scene completely out of her head. She had guests to attend to and entertain. She didn't have time to dwell on Candace's silly trumped-up notions.

But just as Courtney stepped into the hall, she stopped, a devious smile appearing about her lips.

Although Candace's notion was ridiculous, it did have some merit, some plausibility. And it might be useful for Courtney and Nick to let Candace keep her false assumptions alive for a while. Just long enough to make her jealous, make her want Nick as badly as Nick wanted her.

Then Courtney had second thoughts and shook her head. Nah, a scheme like that wouldn't work. Candace wasn't the predatory type; she would back out of the running before the race even began. In fact, she wouldn't even enter. And then what kind of a game would they have?

No, better to keep it all honest and aboveboard, Courtney decided as she headed up the stairs to the living room. She would forget about pretending to be the other woman in Nick's life and just concentrate on doing her best to help him snare Candace. Those two deserved each other.

"More than they'll ever know," she muttered, smiling.

7

As Candace walked out of the women's rest room Shelly, wearing a wide-eyed smile, intercepted her.

"You've got flowers," she said. "And it's not even your birthday."

"Flowers?"

"Roses, Candy. Beautiful, long-stemmed red roses."

Roses? Another bouquet of roses flashed through Candace's mind; the ones she had received for her birthday, just over a month ago. An image of their sender also appeared. Had he sent her this latest batch as well? She prayed that he hadn't. She prayed that Don had.

"Was a card attached?" Candace asked hesitantly.

"Yeah, but I didn't read it," Shelly said. "I figured that since they were your roses, you should have the honor of opening the envelope. But you'd better hurry up and find out who sent them. The whole office is buzzing about it. Even Dr. Hardesty, if you can believe it."

"*My* Dr. Hardesty?" Candace turned away from the bathroom and headed down the long, barren hall to her department. "Dr. Susan Hardesty?"

Shelly nodded, grinning as she kept pace with Candace's long stride. "I was shocked, too. I tell you, if I didn't know better, I'd swear she was jealous of you, Candy."

"No, not Dr. Hardesty. She isn't the jealous type. She's too brainy, too analytical to have ordinary human feelings like jealousy."

Yet when Candace walked through the door of her department, through the small reception area to her office, the first person she saw was Susan Hardesty. The good doctor, wearing the prerequisite white lab coat over her clothes, sensible white shoes, and with her brown hair swept up into a neat little bun at the back of her neck, had her nose buried in one of the lush red blooms.

"They're intoxicating," Susan murmured, catching sight of Candace. "Beautifully intoxicating."

"They are pretty, aren't they?" Candace retrieved the card from the florist's pick as she slipped behind her desk.

"I'd give my right arm for someone to send me roses like these," Susan said.

"Me too," Shelly said. "Who are they from?"

Candace saw Nick's signature on the card, read his brief invitation, and felt her stomach twist into knots. The jerk, she thought.

"Oh, just a friend." She put the card inside the envelope, then stuck it back in the flowers.

"I'd say more than 'just a friend,'" Susan said. "They're from a man, aren't they? A special man."

"Don?" Shelly asked.

"No, not Don." But Candace wished with all her heart

that they had been from him. She hadn't heard from him since he last breezed through town, and she was beginning to think that he had lost interest in her—if he had ever had any interest to begin with, that is. "They're from a guy I met a few months ago, when my friend Ellie got married."

Both Susan and Shelly stood quietly, with expectant expressions, waiting for Candace to elaborate. When she remained silent, Shelly's curiosity forced her to speak up. "And?"

"And nothing," Candace said. "He's just a guy. He's living in Dallas now, we had dinner together the other night, and—"

"Having dinner out together constitutes much more than a mere nothing," Susan said.

"Yeah," Shelly said in agreement. "And stop calling him 'just a guy.' Like Dr. Hardesty said, when someone sends you flowers like this, they're more than 'just' anything. They're someone special. Tell us about him, Candy. Where'd he take you to eat? Someplace fancy and outrageously expensive, I'll bet. Someplace like the Mansion on Turtle Creek, or the French Room at the Adolphus Hotel. Is it serious between you two?"

"He didn't take me anywhere," Candace said. "We had dinner at a friend's house, not a fancy, expensive restaurant. And no, it's not serious between us. To tell you the truth, I barely even know the man." And what she did know of Nick, she didn't like. He may have started out as a nice, likable kind of guy, but he was rapidly becoming a two-timing jerk. Nice guys didn't try to have their cake and eat it, too.

"It looks to me like he wants all that to change," Shelly said, bending over the flowers and sniffing a bloom. "Mmm! If they could only bottle this stuff, they'd make a fortune."

"They have bottled it," Susan said.

Shelly gave her a disbelieving look. "Really?"

Susan nodded. "It's called Joy, and the last time I checked, it was one of the most expensive perfumes you could buy. Of course, that's been a few months ago. They may have something more expensive by now."

"It can't smell as good as these do," Shelly said.

"It does. In fact, the fragrance is almost identical." Susan lowered her head to take another whiff. "My ex-husband bought me a bottle just before he told me he was moving out of the house."

"You're married?" Shelly asked, astonished by the doctor's admission.

"Not for much longer," Susan said, grinning slyly. "When my divorce is final next month, I'll be footloose and fancy-free again."

Shelly and Candace exchanged similar looks. It was amazing what you could learn by keeping your mouth shut and your ears open, Candace thought. All this time she had thought Susan Hardesty was nothing more than a hard-nosed research scientist, like the guys in the lab, merely a brain with no feminine emotions at all. How wrong she had been.

The phone rang, interrupting her musings.

"I guess that's my cue to get back to work," Shelly said.

"Yes, time for me to attend to my little mice, too." Susan gave one last longing look at the floral arrangement and then disappeared through a door.

Finally alone, Candace sat down and picked up the receiver. "R and D. Ms. McFarren speaking."

"How businesslike you sound. Did you get my flowers?"

Nick's deep voice washed over her like a warm velvet wave. "Yes, I got them," she said, wishing he didn't have such a seductive effect on her. She wanted to hate him, but when he talked to her in his low voice, all she could think of, all she could feel, was him, his gentleness, and how wonderful he had been the night they spent together.

"Did you read the card?"

"Yes."

"And?"

"And the answer is no, Nick, I can't have dinner with you?"

"Why not?"

"I just can't, that's all."

"Are you busy tomorrow night? Because if you are, I don't have any problem with us making it the night after."

Candace gritted her teeth, striving for some semblance of control. That was the problem—them *making it*. They had already made it, much to her regret. And as much as she might be tempted to give in to him, to accept his dinner invitation, she couldn't. She had to remain cold and aloof and, above all, calm. But in her frame of mind, calmness remained elusive. The urge to tell him what she thought of him was too overpowering. But she knew that she couldn't lose all restraint and tell him what she really thought of him and his suggestion; ladies didn't use profanity. And besides, she knew that if she ever once started venting her spleen, her voice would increase in volume and the R&D staff would come running out of the lab to investigate. That would never do.

She took a deep breath. "Nick, I think it's best that

we don't see each other again. Ever.''

The deep rumble of laughter she heard in the receiver had the effect of dissipating her anger rather than increasing it. He had laughed that way once before, just moments after they had made love, when he had been so pleased with himself and her response to him.

"Candy, honey, you don't really mean that, do you?"

"Yes, I really do."

"You never want to see me again?"

"That's right, never."

"Candy, Candy, Candy," he said on a long patient sigh.

Nick, Nick, Nick, she thought. Don't do this to me.

"Why?" he asked.

"Why do you think?"

He paused a moment, making a soft clicking sound with his tongue, as if mulling over his response. "I don't really know for sure, but the only answer I can come up with is that you're afraid it might not be as good between us the second time as it was the first."

At the mention of how good they had been together, how so utterly natural, an involuntary warmth began to spread slowly through Candace. They hadn't been good, they had been terrific, fabulous, absolutely extraordinary. She knew that measuring on a scale of one to ten, they had hit an all-time high of fifteen. Making love with Nick had been one of the truly great highlights of her life thus far. And for a brief instant in time, despite the insincere words he had spoken at the time, he had made her feel like a complete woman, not just some brainless blond bimbo with a hot bod, as most men perceived her.

But suddenly reality came rushing back when Candace got a clear mental image of Courtney. "That's not the reason."

"Then what is, honey?"

His endearment ripped through her like a sharp-bladed knife. "Courtney," she said.

"What about her?"

"You tell me, Nick."

"You know more about her than I do. She's your best friend. I only met her a few months ago."

"You only met me a few months ago, too, but you didn't let that stop you, did you?"

"Stop me from what? Going to bed with you? Making love with you? I won't apologize for that, Candy. It happened, and frankly, I'm glad."

"What about Courtney? Is she glad, too, or doesn't she mind sharing your . . . affections?"

"Sharing my what?"

"Your affections, Nick. Or, to put it more simply, your body."

Candace heard dead silence for a moment, then a dry chuckle.

"Are you implying what I think you're implying?"

"I'm not implying a thing. You may be inferring something, but that's your problem, not mine. I'm merely asking a simple question. And if it's not too much trouble, I'd appreciate a straight answer."

"Okay. You want straight talk, you'll get it. I haven't shared anything of mine with Courtney. Not my affections and certainly not my body. In other words, Candy, my sweet, I've never slept with her, gone to bed with her, made love with her, or any other euphemism currently in vogue. Hell, I've never even made a pass at her. I have talked to her—lots of times. I like her. She's a nice lady and easy to like."

I'll bet, Candace thought. "If you don't mind my saying so, I find all that a little hard to believe."

"I don't care if you believe it or not. It's the truth, Candy."

Just at that moment Dr. Franklin walked through Candace's door. She looked up and saw the tapes he carried in his hand. Time for her to cut the conversation short with Nick and go to work.

"Yes, perhaps it is, and perhaps it isn't," she said, pointing a finger to let Dr. Franklin know that she would be with him in a moment. "Look, I'm sorry, but I have to go now. I'm needed here, rather urgently."

Nick chuckled. "I understand, honey. I'll be here whenever you want me."

That was the problem, Candace thought as she hung up the receiver and took the tapes from Dr. Franklin's outstretched hand. She wanted Nick already. But at the same time she didn't want him at all. Not only was he a danger to her fragile ego, he was a very bad influence.

"She actually came right out and asked you that point-blank?" Courtney stirred artificial sweetener into the glass of iced tea Nick had just given to her.

"Yep," he said. "She hit me right between the eyes with it. I'll be honest with you, Court, I didn't know whether to laugh at her or start yelling." He shrugged. "Naturally I took the coward's way out and laughed."

"Then you're no different from me. I did the very same thing. Well, actually mine was more of a stunned giggle than an outburst of laughter."

"Get out of here! Are you saying she confronted you, too, with her cockamamie notion?"

Courtney nodded. "The night of my party. You remember, Candy and I went down into the kitchen to get the cake and coffee?"

Nick couldn't believe what he had just heard. "Son

of a—what has gotten into that woman, anyway? I mean, it's one thing to distrust me, but to assume that I'm going with you while at the same time I'm trying to get a date with her . . . It's stupid.''

"Maybe so, but she's confused, Nick.''

"No kidding.'' Confused and slightly out of her mind, he thought. He hadn't had eyes for any other woman but her since he'd met her.

"But that's exactly the way you wanted her, isn't it?'' Courtney asked.

"No, as I recall, that's the way you said I should get her. How did you put it? Oh yeah. 'Get her confused and keep her off balance for a while—' ''

"And then go in for the kill,'' Courtney said. "Yes, that's what I said, all right.''

"So, are you saying that it's now time for us to start playing this game by my rules, to load up all my live ammo into the heavy artillery? No offense, but playing by your rules hasn't gotten me much headway.'' If anything, he thought, Courtney's rules had put him even farther behind.

Courtney sighed. "Now that you mention it, now might be a very good time to start taking some action. Get a little more aggressive with her. But keep the action positive.''

"Thank God,'' Nick said, getting to his feet and crossing the living room to Courtney. "Aggressive, I can handle. It may not be my middle name, but it's at least within my realm of comprehension. All this passive business of yours has put me a little on edge, I don't mind telling you.''

"Just, please, play it cautiously with her, would you? Candy's very sensitive. I don't want to see her get hurt.''

Grinning, Nick leaned down and hugged Courtney.

"I'm strictly a kid-gloves kind of guy, Court. I won't leave a bruise on her, I swear."

Courtney scowled at him. "You'd better not. You do, and you'll have me to answer to."

"Trust me. I know what I'm doing."

Candace sat on her couch, watching a movie on cable. She had seen it many times before and almost knew the dialogue by heart, but there was something about Harrison Ford that made her want to watch it again and again. Or, rather, watch *him* again and again.

A knock sounded at her door, and she glanced at it. Who would be coming to see her at this time of night? she wondered, padding barefoot across the room.

Living in a security-controlled complex and trusting the computers as she trusted her neighbors, she avoided the use of the safety chain and opened the door. But she felt the urge to shut it again when she saw Nick standing on the landing outside, the small carriage lamp affixed to the wall nearby making his charming boyish smile look almost devilish.

Candace groaned. "I thought you understood me earlier today when I told you that I didn't want to see you again."

"Oh, I understood you, all right," he said, brushing past her with a soft rustle as he entered her apartment. "Your meaning came through loud and clear."

"Then what are you doing here?"

"Well, you see, honey, I don't happen to agree with you. I know how you think you feel, but your feelings at this point really don't matter. Mine, however, do. And I feel we should continue seeing each other, so I decided to come over anyway."

"Well, you've made a wasted trip. I'm not going to

have dinner with you. I've already eaten. And even if I hadn't, it's too late to go out. I've got to go to work tomorrow.''

"So do I. But I'm not here to take you out.''

"Then what are you here for?'' she asked skeptically.

A circular movement of his arm revealed the paper bag that he had been hiding behind his back. With a twist of his wrist, he removed the bottle of wine from inside it. ''I'm here to straighten out a few of your misguided conceptions. Where do you keep your wineglasses? In a kitchen cabinet?''

"I don't have any wineglasses, and what misguided conceptions are you talking about?''

"No wineglasses?''

"No. I don't drink, so I have no use for them.''

"Then I guess we'll have to make do with iced-tea glasses. The wine won't taste quite the same, but I suppose we can manage. Where do you keep them?''

Candace heaved a heavy sigh of frustration. What was she going to do with Nick? She couldn't very well throw him out; he was almost twice as big as she was. And she was too tired to think of ways to talk him into leaving. It seemed to her that the only recourse she had left was to let him have his say and then maybe he would go home and leave her alone.

"The glasses are in the right-hand cupboard, beside the sink.''

He pivoted gracefully on the balls of his feet, keeping his back straight, and peered into her kitchen. "Gotcha.''

"But only get one glass for yourself. Don't get one for me.''

"Are you sure? It's a very good Chardonnay. Dry, but not the least bit assuming.''

"Whatever that means,'' she mumbled. "Yes, I'm

sure, Nick. I don't want any."

"I really prefer not to drink alone."

"Then go take yourself and your unassuming Chardonnay over to Court's," she said beneath her breath. "I'm sure she'd appreciate it."

Flopping back down on the couch, she grabbed a nearby throw pillow and cuddled it to her as she curled her bare feet beneath her.

"What did you say?" Nick called out from the kitchen.

"Nothing," Candace said. "I didn't say anything. It must have been the TV you heard."

Nick grinned as he poured a small measure of wine into a tall glass. It hadn't been the TV he'd heard; it had been Candace, and her jealousy had come through quite clearly.

"What are you watching?" he asked, coming back into the living room and sitting down so close beside her that she scooted further away.

Candace gestured to the screen. "Harrison Ford."

"Oh, yeah, I've seen this one. It's pretty good."

"Good? It's terrific."

"Then you've seen it, too?"

"Yeah, about half a dozen times."

Before she could stop him, Nick grabbed her remote control off the coffee table and turned off the set. "Then you won't be missing anything while we talk." Instead of putting the remote back on the coffee table, he slipped it beneath the cushion beside him.

Surprise at his audacity blended with anger in Candace. "Turn that back on!"

"No."

"Turn it back on, Nick. I was watching that movie."

"But you've already seen it half a dozen times, you said so yourself."

"I don't care. I want to see it again."

"Not tonight. We need to talk, get a few things ironed out."

If she ironed out anything, it would be his head, she thought, her lips folding into a thin, straight line as her eyes narrowed. "Give me back my remote. I'm going to finish watching that movie."

"You can't watch TV and talk to me at the same time, honey."

"So, go home. Nobody asked you to come over. And don't call me honey."

"I know you didn't ask me over. That's the problem. If I waited for you to invite me, there's a strong chance I'd die of old age."

She fought down the temptation to wrestle the remote control from him, but she knew she would lose, so she didn't bother. If he wanted to play the bully, let him. But if he thought she was going to talk to him, he had another think coming.

"Now then," he said, slipping off his loafers and propping his feet up on the coffee table, "about these misguided conceptions of yours."

Candace hugged the throw pillow more tightly to her chest and stared sullenly at the blank TV screen.

"You're all wrong, Candy. I know I've told you that before, but I think it needs repeating, just to get the point across."

Nick waited for her to say something—contradict him, yell at him, take a swing at him, anything. But when she said nothing, he knew he needed to apply a little more pressure with a lot more oomph to get her to open up.

"Courtney is one good-looking woman." He didn't have to touch Candace to see her tension increase. It radiated across the few feet that separated them on the couch. "She's intelligent, a gifted hostess, a better-than-average cook, probably a dynamite lawyer, and one of these days I'm sure she's going to make some man very happy. But that man won't be me. He'll never be me, Candy."

"Yeah, sure." The moment she muttered the sarcastic-sounding words, Candace wanted to kick herself. She had responded to his remark when she had intended to give him the cold shoulder, not to say anything at all to him for the duration of his stay.

"He won't, Candy. I mean it. I like her, sure. I like her a lot, but I don't love her."

Candace turned then, slowly, giving him a look that Nick clearly read.

"You, on the other hand, are a different matter. Remember that night? Our night? Remember what I said?"

"Spare me, Nick. I didn't believe it then, and I won't believe it now. So don't try handing me some tired, worn-out hearts-and-flowers line about how I'm the only girl in your life, the only one you'll ever love, because I won't buy it."

"Not even if it's the truth?"

"No. Because I know it's not the truth. We had a one-night thing, and that's all, so cut this out, would you? I may be gullible and naive where some things are concerned, but not about something as serious as that. Believe it or not, I do know a line when I hear one."

"You've heard a lot of them from guys, is that what you're saying?"

"I've had my fair share, yes," she said, nodding slowly, her face etched with firm determination. What did he think she was, some protected old maid who didn't know the meaning of life, who didn't know the risks that one had to take simply to live it? Well, she wasn't. She knew what life was about, and even though it had dealt her some pretty rough blows, she wasn't about to knuckle under the strain.

"From guys you cared about?"

"No, from total strangers," she shot back snidely. "Of course from guys I cared about." Or guys she had thought she cared about. Looking back on it now, though, she knew she hadn't cared. But at the time, their desertion had hurt. It had hurt a lot.

"Have there been many of them?"

The audacity of the man! she thought, feeling like screaming and throwing something at him. He had no right to come waltzing into her home and pry into her personal life, just because they had spent one night together. "That's none of your business, Nick."

"Wrong, Candy. It is my business."

She turned sharply on the couch to face him, still clutching the pillow in front her, her short nails digging so hard into the fabric that her knuckles turned white. "Look, whatever I've done in the past, and who I've done it with, is solely my business. You got that?"

"That may have been so at one time, but not anymore."

She gnashed her teeth in angry frustration. "Why, you—"

"Stop right there," he said, holding up a silencing hand. "Before you go any further, let me explain. All right, granted, your past is yours; you have to live with it the rest of your life. But what I'm trying to say, what I'm trying to get across to you is that your past is mine now, too."

"Who says?"

"I say. When you chose to go to bed with me that

night, here in this very apartment, you made it mine. And by the same token, my past became yours.''

Candace snorted in disbelief. ''For heaven's sake, Nick. We slept together. That's all. We weren't surgically joined at the hip.''

''The connection may not be visible, but it's there, Candy. Believe me, it's there. Want me to prove it to you?'' He leaned toward her slightly, his arm sliding along the back of the couch, his hand inching ever closer to her shoulder.

Candace arched her back, moving away from him. ''Don't come any closer.''

''Why not?''

''I don't want you to touch me, that's why not.''

''Are you afraid to find out that I'm right? I am, you know.''

''I know nothing of the kind. You come over here tonight, uninvited, after I've told you I don't want to see you, and you start playing some kind of psychological game with me. What's the matter, was Courtney too busy to see you or something?''

Nick expelled a tired sigh and moved back to his corner of the couch. ''Leave Courtney out of this, would you? She has nothing to do with it. This is strictly between you and me.''

''Wrong,'' Candace said. ''There's nothing between you and me. Not this, not anything.'' Nothing but their one night together that she wished she could forget. But she couldn't forget it, mainly because Nick and his damned stubborn persistence wouldn't let her.

''There could be, if you'd only give us a chance.''

His voice, so soft yet so coercive, so seductively believable, made her stop for a moment to consider what he'd said. Did they really have a chance, even a remote one? Could they begin a relationship and sustain it long enough for it to develop into something other than the animal attraction that had brought them together in the first place?

Though greatly intrigued by the possibility, not to mention tempted, Candace shook her head. "I'm afraid we'd both be wasting our time."

"Why do you say that?"

"We're too different. We have nothing in common."

"Wrong," he said. "We have a lot in common."

"Name one thing. And please, don't bring up the subject of that night."

A slight grin played about Nick's mouth as he surveyed her living room, taking in her small TV, her stereo, her selection of tapes and LPs that she had neatly arranged on a shelf, and the colorful prints that hung on her stark white walls. "We both like to eat. We both like movies. And you must like listening to music, or you wouldn't have that stereo. Funny thing—I like music, too."

Candace shook her head. "Those comparisons are far too general. Just about everybody likes movies, music, and food."

"Ah, but not all the same kind of movies, music, and food."

"Well, be more specific, would you?"

"All right, how about personal fulfillment, a need to be happy, a sense that we've spent our life accomplishing something other than taking up space on this shrinking little planet of ours?"

"That's still too general, Nick."

"No, it's not. You'd be amazed at the number of people who merely exist, who don't take chances, who can't imagine what they're capable of doing because they're too afraid to take a risk.'' People like you, Candy, love, he thought.

Taking chances? Taking risks? She could understand why people wouldn't do those sorts of things. ''I wouldn't be amazed at all. Some people prefer comfort and security to feeling like they're living on the edge all the time. Living like that is much too stressful. It can give you ulcers and put you in an early grave.''

''But where's the joy in living if you don't take a chance once in a while, have a little fun doing it?''

''The joy is in knowing that you're doing your best.''

''Okay. But what about the fun?''

She hesitated. ''That comes as an added bonus.''

''Do you have fun staying on the straight and narrow all the time, never being late for work, never taking a day off when you didn't have it coming to you? Never swerving to the right or left, even for only a moment?''

''Yes, of course I do. That's a silly question.''

Though Candace had responded quickly, without taking much time to consider the question, she couldn't deny that a seed of doubt was forming in the back of her mind. She had worked for the same company for years, since shortly after graduating from college. She had always given the company her very best, always been on time, and had never asked for special privileges, or even a raise in salary when she knew she had one coming to her. She always took what they gave her and didn't make a fuss. But had she had much fun doing her job?

No, in all honesty, she couldn't say she had.

Stop thinking like that, Candace told herself. Stop thinking like Nick.

''Staying on the straight and narrow all the time isn't bad,'' she said. ''As a matter of fact, it's pretty good. You should try it sometime.''

"Living a routine life makes you feel safe, does it?"

"Yes, it does."

"Getting up at the same time of day, eating the same breakfast, driving the same route to work?"

"Yes. There's nothing wrong with that. Nothing at all."

"Not even the traffic jams on the freeways that seem to get worse instead of better?"

"Well, traffic is traffic. There's no way of avoiding it. Nobody likes it; you just have to learn to live with it."

"Not necessarily. You could try taking a different route to work."

"Why?"

He shrugged. "You'd see a change in scenery."

"Sure," she said. "And while I'm tooling along, looking at the scenery, I'm not getting to work on time."

"Have you ever been late?"

"No."

"Not even once?"

"No."

Silently, Nick groaned in frustration. He wasn't making any headway with Candace, no headway at all. She had lived in a rut for so long, had become so used to it, that boredom was a part of her daily routine.

Well, he had to get her out. He had to make her see that life outside her routine was waiting for her, begging her to come and grasp it.

Then suddenly he had an idea. "What do you think your boss would do to you if you were late just one morning?"

"Oh, I don't know." But a little voice in the back of her head told her that Dr. Franklin probably wouldn't do anything at all. He barely acknowledged her presence as it was, even though she was always punctual.

"You don't think they'd fire you, do you?"

"I seriously doubt it. I've got a perfect record at work. Why would they fire me for being late one time?"

"I don't know, just asking," Nick said. "How about taking a day off?"

"You mean a sick day or a day of vacation? I have those coming to me already. They couldn't do anything about that, either."

"Then why not take one?"

"Because for one thing, I always take my vacation in September. And for another, I don't take sick days unless I absolutely need them."

Mischief sparkled in the depths of his dark brown eyes as he inched closer to her. "Call in sick tomorrow."

"What?"

"Call in sick."

"No!"

"Why not?"

"Because I'm not sick, that's why not."

"Your boss won't know that."

"No, but I will."

"Come on, Candy. Take a day off and play hooky with me."

She looked at him like he had suddenly sprouted horns. "No!"

"We could have a lot of fun together."

"Fun, huh?"

"Yeah."

"Nick, I have a feeling that your idea of fun isn't the same as mine."

"How do you know? You've never really given yourself a chance to find out."

"It couldn't be the same," she said, feeling a weakening begin to overtake her firm resolve.

"Give it a shot. I dare you."

"I don't take dares. They're childish."

"How about bets?"

"Bets?"

"Yeah. I'll bet you a home-cooked dinner that by this time tomorrow night, after you've spent the whole day with me, you'll have had more fun than you've had in a long time."

She eyed him skeptically. "Doing what?"

"Anything and everything we want to do."

"Uh-huh, that's what I thought."

"No, not that, Candy," he said, knowing that she thought he was referring to them making love again. It hadn't been the idea he originally had in mind, but now that she had brought it up, he had to admit that it was a nice notion, one he would eagerly initiate if he thought he had a chance.

"Nice try, Nick, but the answer is still no."

"What if I promise not to touch you?"

"No!" Candace didn't trust his promises; they weren't worth the breath he used to speak them.

"I won't lay a hand on you."

His hands, she recalled vividly, were too clever, too quick, and once they started moving, she knew she wouldn't have the emotional or physical wherewithal to stop them. "No, Nick."

"I won't come on to you, either."

"No."

But even Candace could hear the lack of conviction in her tone.

8

CANDACE HADN'T WANTED TO SEE
Nick again. She had firmly believed that once she told
him just how she felt, she would never see him again.
After all, he was an intelligent man; he would have the
sense to know he was wasting his time. And hers.

That's what she had thought.

Yet here she was, not only seeing him, but going out
with him. Worse than that, she had given in to his constant prodding of last night, taking him at his word that
he would not discuss the night they had spent together,
and had called in sick this morning. "Playing hooky
together," as he had called it.

Asking for trouble was more like it, to her way of
thinking.

Way to stick to your convictions, McFarren, she
thought, glancing over at Nick.

He sat behind the steering wheel of his shiny new
pickup truck, humming a country-western song beneath
his breath as he took the Coit Road exit off LBJ Freeway.

Dressed as he was in his cowboy boots and hat, his western shirt and snug jeans, and driving his new truck, no one looking at him would know that he was from New York City. But let him open his mouth and his secret would be out.

"Why the western outfit?" she asked.

"What's the matter, don't you like it?"

Frankly, she did. She liked his new look a lot, but she hesitated to tell him that. He looked too comfortable, so at ease with himself and his surroundings, despite the fact that very few men in Dallas wore western garb, except at home or on special occasions. Two- and three-piece business suits were the standard these days during a work week.

"It's all right, I suppose," she said. "It's just that I couldn't help wondering what made you choose to wear something like that."

"Hey, as they say—when in Rome . . ."

"But wouldn't sneakers and a T-shirt have been more comfortable? Those boots have got to be pinching your feet."

"As a matter of fact, they're pretty comfortable. They were a little tight when I first bought them, but I've pretty much stretched them out by now." He slowed to a stop as they reached the traffic light. "Where is this place you're taking me to?"

"Olla Podrida? It's just up ahead. See that big building on the right that looks like a cross between an airplane hangar and a warehouse?"

"Yeah."

"That's Olla Podrida."

"And that's supposed to be a good place to shop?" Nick sounded doubtful.

"Yes, it is, if you're looking for something that's a

little different, sometimes one-of-a-kind and hand-made,'' Candace said. ''Of course, we could always forget about Olla Podrida and go to Valley View Mall. Or better still, we could go to the Galleria. There's a Saks Fifth Avenue and a Macy's and a Marshall Fields there.''

''Maybe later,'' Nick said, driving off as the light changed. ''I got enough of Saks and Macy's back in New York. I want something that's totally Texas.''

''I'm afraid you'd have to go to Fort Worth for that. You could always visit the Stockyards. But you'd have to go alone. I'm slightly allergic to horses.''

''No, not Fort Worth. I want something that's totally Dallas.''

Candace frowned in confusion. ''I don't think there is such a thing, Nick.'' Dallas was a mixture of the East Coast and the West, accepting both the best and the worst trends from each place, then altering them slightly to fit the sometimes finicky Dallas taste. It may have had its own style at one time, back when Texas was a republic and not just another state, but that had been a long time ago.

''Just what are you looking for, exactly?'' she asked.

''Something with a lot of southwest flavor to it.''

''A rug, a lamp . . . what?''

He shot her a sidelong glance and grinned. ''To be perfectly honest, I'm not really sure, but I'll know it when I see it.''

Nick found a parking place well away from all the other cars in the parking lot.

''Hey, it's a new truck,'' he said when Candace complained of the hike they were going to have to make. ''I want to keep it looking as new as possible for as long as possible. Parking it this far away, no one can open his door and bang it into mine.''

Lucky thing they were here on a weekday when there weren't so many shoppers, Candace thought as they made their way toward the building. On a Saturday or Sunday, the place would probably have been a madhouse.

A pair of unassuming steel doors led into the building, a set of wide wooden stairs on the left climbing to the second level. Nick suggested they take the second story first. Candace followed him, too preoccupied with the lush green hanging ferns and spider plants to object. How did the Olla Podrida staff keep these plants looking so green? she wondered. She had all kinds of direct and indirect light in her apartment, but every plant she'd ever bought and taken home had seemed to wither and die within weeks. Then she looked up and saw the skylights overhead. Perhaps good lighting was the secret.

They reached the landing paved in rich red Mexican tile, then took the second flight to the upper level. As she always did when she shopped at Olla Podrida, Candace found herself salivating at the displays in all the small shops. One sold hand-embroidered dresses and shawls from India, two others sold delicate handmade baby clothes from Ireland and Israel, still another sold all the tools and implements one would need to make homemade wine. Around a corner and through a set of arches that connected the main shopping corridor with its smaller annex, and she found herself in the local and imported handicrafts section.

Stained-glass and leaded windowpanes graced one shop, some with ordinary designs and others so personalized that they had to be custom orders. Down the way a bit, and they came to a shop specializing in brass, pots, urns, and decanters in all shapes and sizes standing on the floor, one large enough to be mistaken for a bathtub.

"Have you seen anything you like yet?" Candace asked as Nick led her back downstairs and into the main shopping corridor. Feeling her feet begin to ache, she realized belatedly that she should have worn sneakers and not low-heeled shoes.

"Nope, not yet."

"Something totally Texas, huh?"

"That's right."

"Well then, come with me. There's a shop down this way that might have the very thing you're looking for."

"I don't want souvenirs, Candy," Nick said as he saw the shop to which she was leading him. "Ashtrays and saltshakers, I've already got. I want something useful, something practical, and at the same time something—"

"I know, totally Texas. I get the idea, Nick."

As they walked past a food stall Candace forced herself to ignore her growling stomach. Nick had promised her a surprise for lunch, but that had been hours ago, when they had first left her apartment.

"Need any cookware?" she asked, pausing by a shop that sold everything from gourmet pots and pans to professional kitchen gadgets.

"No, not really."

"I once saw a skillet in there that was shaped like the state of Texas."

"Really?"

Believing—praying—she detected a note of curiosity in his voice, she pressed on. "Yeah. Who knows? They might still have it."

"Candace, no offense, but I don't want a Texas-shaped skillet."

"But you said you wanted something useful and practical. How useful and practical and patriotic can you get?

It seems to me that a Texas-shaped skillet covers all three.''

Nick turned and gave her a patient smile. "I know you mean well, but a skillet isn't what I'm after. I've already got a skillet. And a sauté pan, and a crêpe pan, and a wok.''

He didn't want a stuffed armadillo, either, she learned moments later after they had browsed through the displays in the souvenir shop. Nor was he too enthusiastic over investing in the set of University of Texas highball glasses she showed him, or the large ceramic ashtray, again shaped like Texas, that said "Shalom Y'all."

She had all but given up hope of him ever finding anything he liked when Nick suddenly froze in his tracks.

"That's it," he said, grinning from ear to ear.

Cautiously, Candace peered around his broad shoulders into the tiny shop, her eyes feasting first on the luxurious quilted bedspread of satin, velvet, and lace in yummy shades of peach and cream. Scattered across the top of the bed were small pillows in every shape and size—lacy hearts and circles, ruffled bolsters—all matching the bedspread.

And then she noticed the bed itself. The four-poster frame consisted of what looked to her like gnarled tree trunks, the two at the foot boasting knotholes in the posts. The headboard resembled an old split-rail fence of the same type of wood, all of the pieces very smooth. All of it probably very expensive, too, she thought.

"That's what you've been looking for? A bed?''

Even Candace heard the note of skepticism in her tone, the note of disbelief. He had promised her last night, on his honor, that he wouldn't come on to her today. Yet here he stood, right beside her, drooling like some idiot over a bed. If that wasn't a come-on, she would like to hear one.

"Yeah. I wonder how much they're asking for it?"

"Probably more than you can afford." More than I could afford, that's for sure, she thought. "That looks like a one-of-a-kind to me. You really ought to try a furniture store."

"I've looked in the furniture stores. They didn't have anything I wanted. But this now . . . this is super." Forgetting he had promised her the night before that he wouldn't touch her, he wrapped a proprietary arm around her waist and led her inside.

"A bed's a bed, Nick."

"No, Candy. This isn't just a bed. It's rustic with a lot of character to it. It says, 'Hey, I'm a Texas bed, and damned proud of it.' "

He thought it would talk to him? Candace felt herself cringe inside. Obviously the man had been out in the sun too long. Either the sun, or he had been cooped up in a badly ventilated room with his paints and ad layouts, and he had gone off the deep end.

"Nick, this bed—furniture in general doesn't talk. It's inanimate."

A woman who looked to be in her mid-thirties stood nearby. Having overheard their conversation, she chuckled. "Not only that, it's not from Texas."

Nick's enthusiasm seemed to waver. "It's not?"

"No, it's from Arizona."

"Well, hey, that's all right. Arizona's the southwest, isn't it?"

"Yes, it is, but I'm afraid this bed's not for sale. I'm just using it for display."

"Oh, I'm sorry," Nick said. "I thought you were just

another customer, looking around. I didn't know you worked here."

The woman smiled. "I do a lot more than work here. I'm the owner/manager of this space."

"You have some very lovely merchandise," Candace said, tugging gently on Nick's arm in hopes that he would get her unspoken hint that they leave. "But as you no doubt heard, it seems he's got his heart set on a bed. Come on, Nick. Let's go."

"No," he said. "Now that I've found what I've been looking for, I'll do whatever it takes to get it."

"But, Nick, didn't you just hear her? She's not going to sell it."

"I couldn't, even if I wanted to," the woman said, lifting the bedspread and showing Nick the base. "You see? It doesn't even have a frame for a mattress and box spring. I've just got a lot of empty cartons stacked beneath it to make it look more like a real bed."

"That's even better," Nick said. "I've already got a king-size frame. I wouldn't have to throw it out or find a place to store it when I set this one up."

"Nick," Candace said, "listen to her carefully. This bed is not for sale."

He turned then, smiling down at her, and she noted how his dark brown eyes glittered with excitement, just like he was playing some kind of game and loving every minute of it. Candace felt her knees turn to rubber. She had seen that look in his eyes once before, merely moments before she had succumbed to his wily charms, his silkily spoken words. Only this time it seemed to be the salesclerk's turn, not hers.

Nick looked back at the woman, his smile growing warmer, more seductive.

Candace, unable to believe Nick's audacity, glanced

at the woman, certain that she would see someone professional, who knew her own mind, who wouldn't knuckle
under to Nick's flirtatious guile. After all, you couldn't
own and operate your own business for as long as this
woman seemed to have run hers and not know something
about remaining steadfast in your beliefs. But instead of
seeing the woman shake her head, Candace watched a
blush slowly creep into her cheeks, and she knew in an
instant who the winner of this brief skirmish would be.

"I really want this bed," Nick said earnestly. "It's
exactly what I've been looking for."

"I can see that," the woman said. "I'll tell you what—
perhaps I could give you the name of the man I bought
it from out in Arizona. You could call him and see if he
has one in stock. Or if he doesn't, he might make one
just like it for you. I'm sure he's still in the business. I
only got it a couple of years ago."

"That's a very good idea, Miss . . . ?"

"Boatwright. *Mrs.* Shirley Boatwright."

"That's a very good idea, Shirley, but I've got an
even better idea. Why don't I buy this bed from you,
and include a little extra in the check to cover the cost
of you getting a replacement for it."

Turn him down, Shirley, tell him no, Candace
screamed in silent desperation. Don't let him have the
bed.

But Shirley merely smiled. "Now, why didn't I think
of that?"

"You would have, if you were as desperate as I am,"
Nick said, pulling out his wallet full of credit cards.

Desperate? Candace thought with a visible smirk. Try
despicable, Nick. Absolutely and utterly despicable.

* * *

"Business is business," Nick said sometime later as they drove down the twisting, turning, tree-lined streets of east Dallas, the part of town that he now thought of as home. "She's out to make a dollar, and today she made quite a few of them, thanks to me."

"Well, if I had been her, I wouldn't have given you that bed."

"She didn't give me anything, Candy. She sold me part of her merchandise. It's mine now, bought and paid for. I've got the receipt to prove it and everything. Good old Shirley and I made the deal, fair and square."

"Fair? There was nothing at all fair about it, Nick. You"—Candace groped for the right word—"you bamboozled her out of that bed, and you know it."

"Bamboozled?"

"Yeah, conned, hoodwinked."

"I didn't do that—any of it."

"Yes, you did. I was standing right beside you when you did it. I heard every word you said, and I saw you with my own two eyes. Honestly, did you have to lay the old Giulianni charm on her so thick? Chances are the poor woman will be scraping it off for months to come."

Believing he detected a note of jealousy in Candace's voice, Nick smiled. The notion that she could be jealous of another woman didn't just please him, it delighted him to no end. Even remembering how she had misunderstood about his relationship with Courtney made him feel slightly giddy inside. Damn it, it meant that she cared. Candace, he thought, could protest all she wanted—she could proclaim until she was blue in the face that she never wanted to see him again—he now knew differently.

A slight frown creased his forehead. He wondered if he could utilize Candace's jealousy to his benefit later, when the time was right. He sincerely hoped so.

"Is that your way of saying I'm charming?"

"No!" Candace said. "Certainly not."

"But you just said—"

"I said you charmed that woman into all but giving you that bed. I didn't say one word about you being charming. The two may be closely related in meaning, but in this case they're entirely different."

Nick suppressed an amused chuckle. "If you say so."

"I do."

"End of subject?"

Not by a long shot, buster, Candace thought. He might be able to charm salesclerks out of their exorbitantly high-priced store displays, but he wasn't about to charm her again. She wouldn't let him. If it took all the energy she possessed, she would make sure that she never fell victim to his seductive spell again, his softly spoken words, his oh-so-gentle caresses . . .

"Yeah," she said, determination evident in her tone. "End of subject."

"Okay, then how about some lunch? I don't know about you, but all this shopping has given me an appetite."

"Sure, lunch sounds fine."

Lunch, Candace said to herself. The reason she was with him today, when she had thoroughly intended never to see him again. The reason she had called in to work that morning and told them she was sick, when in reality, she had never felt better in her life. Worse than that, it was the reason why she might become a member of the unemployed if Dr. Franklin ever discovered her duplicity. She was risking everything she had worked so hard for, and all because he didn't want to eat alone.

Yeah, McFarren, what a way to stick to your convictions, she thought as Nick turned his new pickup off Garland Road, past the open wrought-iron gates, and into the private drive of what once had been the De Golyer Estate. He had done it to her again, she realized. He had charmed her—no, he had seduced her into doing what he wanted. And damn it, like some weak-minded female who couldn't say no, she had let him.

"I thought we could have a nice, quiet lunch here," he said, pulling the truck to a stop in the parking lot of the Dallas Arboretum and Botanical Gardens. "Looks like I was wrong. All these people can't be having lunch. Wonder what's going on?"

Candace wrenched herself out of her angry musings and looked around. Nearby, two young mothers were loading four children into a station wagon—two babies, still in strollers, and two toddlers. Off in the distance, in the heart of the garden, surrounded by shade trees and colorful flowers, a bride and groom stood before a minister. Around then mingled a score or more of well-dressed onlookers. Closer by, women in summery dresses and big hats ambled slowly down the walkways between well-tended flower beds.

"It's Dallas Blooms," she said.

"Dallas Blooms?" Nick nodded. "Okay. That tells me a whole lot."

Candace sighed. "Dallas Blooms is our annual flower show. Every type of flower, tree, or shrub that can be grown in this area at this time of year is on display. People come by and look at them and get ideas for what they would like to put in their gardens."

Nick glanced off at the wedding party, watching a moment as the bride wound her arms around the groom's neck and kissed him. "People get married at flower shows down here?" Back where he was from, most of the people he knew either got married in church or city hall.

"Sure," she said. "It's a pretty place to have a wedding, don't you think? The grass is neatly cut, the flowers are all in bloom, and you couldn't ask for more perfect weather. Why not get married here?"

"Yeah, why not?" He opened the door of the truck and stepped out. "Are you sure they won't object to us having a picnic?"

"No, they won't object. They've got some tables over near the Garland Road entrance just for picnickers. And as long as we clean up our mess and leave the place the way we found it, I don't see why they should object."

They hadn't objected last year, Candace recalled, when she had picnicked on the grounds with Court and Ellie. Of course, a lot could happen in a year's time; the gardens' policy could have changed. Come to think of it, a lot *had* happened. Ellie had married and moved away and had started a new life for herself in New York City with Tony, her new husband. Court seemed more remote than ever. But that was probably due to the fact that she had a heavy, demanding caseload.

Oddly enough, though, nothing much had happened to Candace in the past twelve months. She still had the same job, worked the same hours, saw the same people. She still lived in the same tiny one-bedroom apartment, drove the same car to work every day along the same congested route, and waited for the same man, Don, to make up his mind about their future together. Nick was the only new addition to her life, and she wasn't at all sure yet if that was a change for the better or the worse.

Her life certainly hadn't been boring since he had reentered it, she decided as they carried Nick's wicker picnic hamper and insulated cooler toward the picnic tables. If anything, he had managed to spice it up considerably. In fact, he had come very close a time or two to turning it completely upside down, as he had done when she had first met him. But that, she realized, was mostly her fault, not his.

9

"*I* HOPE YOU LIKE ITALIAN FOOD," Nick said as he opened the hamper and produced a red-checked tablecloth.

They had found a table beneath the shady branches of an oak tree, and even though they were close to the street and could see the traffic speeding by through the hedges, Candace felt as if they were alone, almost secluded.

"I like just about anything, as long as it's not too hot and spicy." She watched as he removed real plates and flatware, not paper or plastic ones, two wineglasses, and some covered bowls from the hamper.

"How about red wine?"

For an answer, Candace merely let her face contort slightly as she made an objectionable sound.

"Don't tell me you don't drink."

"I'm afraid I don't."

"Why not? Is it against your religion or something?" Nick opened the insulated cooler, filled with crushed ice, and produced a bottle of red wine. He found a corkscrew in the lid of the hamper and applied it to the top of the bottle, turning it with a well-practiced twist of his wrist until the grooves had disappeared down inside the cork.

"No, it's just that I've never really developed a taste for the stuff."

"But you have had wine in the past, haven't you?"

"Oh, sure. Don't you remember? I had a little glass of champagne at Tony and Ellie's wedding."

"No, I can't say that I do." The only thing Nick could clearly recall from that evening was his preoccupation with Candace. He had been too busy watching her and her so-called boyfriend, Don, and how they interacted with each other. He hadn't paid any attention to what kind of alcohol she had or had not been consuming.

"Trust me, I had some," Candace said.

The tone of her voice answered his question before he even asked it. "Didn't you like it?"

"No, as a matter of fact, I didn't."

"What was wrong with it?"

"Well, for one thing it was too strong, and for another it gave me a headache. But that's not surprising. Most of the wine I've ever drunk has given me a headache." She shrugged slightly. "I don't know—maybe it's just that my system isn't able to tolerate it."

"Then again, maybe you just haven't tried the right wine yet."

"Maybe I haven't." She watched as he pulled the cork out of the bottle and poured the clear, dark red liquid into one of the glasses.

"Try this and tell me what you think," he said.

Reluctantly, she took the glass from him and sipped it. Almost immediately her face twisted into a grimace, and she shuddered as the bitterness of the liquid attacked her tongue and throat. Without a word or a second thought, she handed the glass back to Nick.

"You don't like it?"

Candace shook her head. "Thanks all the same, and no offense, but you can keep your wine. I'd rather have a diet Coke or a glass of iced tea."

"I didn't buy any Coke, and I didn't make any iced tea," he said, delving down into the cooler again. "I didn't think it would be necessary. Would a ginger ale do instead?"

"Ginger ale would be fine."

Once he had poured ginger ale into the remaining empty wineglass, Nick proceeded to uncover the bowls he had brought, halving their contents onto each of the two plates. Fresh pasta salad with minced black olives, artichoke hearts, and tiny asparagus spears rested along-side rolls of prosciutto and cheese. Crusty garlic bread completed the main course.

"Have you always lived in Dallas?" he asked when the meal had gotten under way, and he saw that she liked what he had prepared.

"No, not always. I was born in Longview. Do you know where that's at?"

He hesitated a moment, more interested in watching the way she took tiny bites of the food, letting her moist pink lips close over the fork before slowly pulling it out. The woman was an innocent sadist; she had no idea that the simple way she ate was driving him crazy.

"Longview?" he asked, dragging himself back to the topic at hand. "No, I can't say that I do."

"It's east of here. Not far, about two hours or so along the interstate."

"Is it a small town or large one?"

"Compared to Dallas, it's very small, but it's still a pretty good-sized place."

"Why did you leave there?"

A faint smile touched her lips. "I really didn't have much choice. I was only two at the time, and when my parents moved here, I sort of had to move with them."

Nick nodded. "Any brothers or sisters?"

She wondered why he was giving her the third degree, and then the answer came to her. He was trying to get to know her better. Despite the fact that they had slept together once months ago, they were still virtually strangers. He knew very little about her, and she knew even less about him.

"Lots of them," she said, deciding that answering his questions wouldn't hurt. If anything, it might make him understand her more clearly, make him realize why she couldn't see him again.

"I've got four—three sisters and a brother," he said. "How many have you got?"

"Five sisters and two brothers. Counting me, there's eight of us altogether."

"Eight?"

"That's right."

"It must get kind of chaotic for you around Christmas and holidays."

Slowly, Candace shook her head. "It doesn't get chaotic at all. You see, technically, I'm an only child. My mother and father had no other children together but me. The other seven are all half-brothers and half-sisters, and I'm the only one who lives in Dallas. Everybody else lives either in New Mexico or Waco."

"Your parents are divorced?"

"Mmm-hmm. Mom remarried when I was ten. She and Lloyd, her husband, and their two sons, lived in Dallas until just before I graduated from high school. That's when Lloyd got offered a teaching position at

Baylor University. He took it, and they moved.

"My dad's got a different story, though. He remarried the first time when I was about five, had a couple of daughters with Irene, and when she died in a car accident, he waited a couple of years and then married Berniece. They've got three little girls. Well, five girls, counting the first two he had with Irene."

"When did all this happen? I mean, how old were you when your parents divorced?"

"Three."

The thought of Candace at three, such a tender, impressionable age, hit Nick hard. What she must have gone through, how she must have felt. How she must feel now. Both her mother and father all but gone from her life, living their own lives elsewhere with new families.

His parents had been married for almost forty years now, and while they had their rocky moments, as most married couples do at one time or another, they always managed to work through the tough times and stick together. In his family, divorce was an unthinkable subject.

If and when he ever got married, divorce would be unthinkable to him as well. For him, it would be "till death do us part."

Candace spoke up, breaking into his thoughts.

"I'm not real sure, but the way Mom tells it, Daddy decided after a while that Dallas didn't quite equal his expectations, so that's when he moved to New Mexico."

"He left you and your mother, walked out, just like that?"

"Oh, no. He divorced her first." With anyone else, Candace wouldn't have dreamed of discussing her parents' lives, past or present. But for reasons she couldn't explain, she didn't mind discussing this with Nick. He was different. She could sense that he honestly cared, that his interest in her background wasn't triggered by maliciousness, but by ordinary curiosity.

"Or was it Mom who divorced Dad?" Frowning with uncertainty, she shrugged. "Actually, I'm not too sure who divorced whom. After all, I was only three at the time. I don't remember much about what happened back then. Not that it makes a whole lot of difference now."

So many questions began racing through Nick's head, he didn't know which one to ask first. Had her parents argued? Had they fought, physically? Had they put Candace in the middle, using her as a pawn as they lashed out at one another? Or had it been something entirely different that had broken them up? Had each of them found someone else?

"So your mom stayed on here in Dallas, instead of going back to Longview?"

"Yeah, she had to," Candace said. "If she had gone back, she wouldn't have had anyone but me. See, she had no family. No parents—they'd both been dead for years before I was even born. No brothers and sisters, aunts or uncles, no cousins. Anyway, we couldn't very well pack up and move. She had a lot of responsibilities, not the least of which was her job. She wasn't a professional woman or anything—just a secretary like I am now, but we made out okay."

No, you didn't, Nick thought. You didn't make out okay at all.

Candace's mother might have been content with the divorce, but Nick could clearly see that Candace had been miserable. She had been three years old and separated from her father, far too young to know why he had left her. And with her mother working long hours, she had to have been frightened and unsure half the time.

Poor little kid. No wonder her self-esteem was still in the toilet.

"Where I come from, Candy, secretaries are considered professionals. They may not make as much as their bosses, but they're just as important. And in some instances they carry almost as much clout." Nick knew that much from experience. More than once in his career as an advertising executive, he had come across secretaries who had been harder to get past than the security guard at the front door. And not only had they been protective of their employers, they had had major decision-making responsibilities.

"Do you have a secretary?"

"Me?" Nick laughed. "Yeah, you're looking at him."

Candace's blue eyes widened in surprise. "You're kidding."

"No, I'm dead serious. And just for the record, I'm not too proud to say that I'm not a very good secretary, either. My files are in a mess." Lines formed into a thoughtful frown on his forehead. "No, that's not exactly true. I don't have any files at all to speak of, now that I think about it. Mostly, I just sort of stack papers in little piles around my office floor."

With Nick being as creative as he was, Candace could believe that. The research scientists that she had worked with for years may not have been ad men, like Nick, but they were still creative in a sense. And she knew firsthand of their personal eccentricities and work habits, which sometimes bordered on just plain slovenliness. Stacks of computer printout sheets, handwritten test results, months-old memos from the head office in the main building, and even remains of old half-eaten lunches could often be found on their desks. Creative people, she decided, just didn't have it in them to be neat.

"If it's that bad," she said, "why don't you hire yourself a secretary?"

"To do what?"

"Well, I don't know. What secretaries are supposed to do, I guess. Answer your mail, pay your bills, make business appointments for you . . . The kinds of things that you have to take time out to do now."

Nick considered her suggestion and nodded. "That would certainly cut back on some of my present responsibilities. But I don't think so."

"Why not?"

"I can't see myself shelling out the added expense. Remember, I'm still working on a limited budget. I will be for a little while longer, by the looks of things."

"But you don't have to hire a full-time secretary. You could call a temporary employment agency and get someone to come in part-time. Just a couple of days a week to start with. She could at least help straighten out your files, make it so you could find things more easily when you need them."

"I don't know," Nick said. "Maybe in a couple of months, when I've got a few additional accounts."

"But what are you going to do about a filing system in the mean time?"

He shrugged. "There's not much I can do, really. I'll just continue to cope, I guess."

Suddenly his back straightened, and he looked squarely at Candace, his brown eyes glittering.

"What?" she asked.

Nick grinned. "I just had a terrific idea."

Candace had never thought of herself as a mind reader, but she didn't have to be one to realize what thoughts were racing through his head. He wanted her to work for him.

"Oh, no. No, Nick, I can't."

"Why not?"

"Because, I already have a job."

"You wouldn't have to work full-time for me."

"No."

"Come on, Candy. You said yourself that all it would take is a couple of days a week to get everything straightened out."

"No, I'm sorry. I couldn't, even if I wanted to." Which she certainly did not. Work for Nick? Be in the same small space with him for hours on end? No, she couldn't and still stay sane.

But then again, Candace decided after a moment's consideration, the notion of earning a little extra money did sound intriguing. She would insist on Nick paying her; she wasn't about to work for him for nothing. And with the extra money, she could start saving for that European vacation she had always wanted, and now badly needed.

"Not even if it was just afternoons or evenings and some weekends?" he asked.

Candace laughed. "You're making it sound like an after-school job. I don't go to school anymore, Nick. I work eight, sometimes ten hours a day. I couldn't work another two or three. I would never have a chance to rest."

"Filing can't be that hard."

"Filing itself isn't. It's setting up the files that's a pain in the neck. Believe me, I know what I'm talking about. Putting together a filing system can take weeks." And in Nick's case, she thought, probably months.

"So, I'm in no rush," he said with an easy grin. "Take all the time you want."

"No."

He reached across the table and took hold of her hand. "Don't be so quick to turn me down, Candy. Think it over."

"I don't need to think it over. I can't do it. I won't do it."

"I think the four-drawer model that we saw back on the other aisle would be better for you," Candace said much later that afternoon as she and Nick prowled through the office-supply store.

They were buying furniture, again. Beds in the morning, office supplies in the afternoon . . . Heaven only knew what Nick would be in the market to buy by the time evening rolled around. Hot tubs and saunas? At this stage of the game, Candace wouldn't be a bit surprised by anything he did.

"Four drawers, huh?"

"That's right."

"Why not just two?" Nick asked, looking at the price tag taped to the top of the smaller cabinet. It was almost half the price of the larger model they had seen moments earlier.

"Because with four drawers, you get twice the amount of file space but you use the exact same amount of floor space as you would with a two. Unless, of course, you decide to take two two-drawer cabinets and stack them, one on top of the other. Even that way, you've still got four. And you're going to need at least a four-drawer cabinet to start with, for all the files and stuff you've got. Who knows, maybe even two four-drawers."

Nick knew he had stacks of papers cluttering his office

floor, but it wasn't so bad that it warranted him going deeply into debt.

"Let's not get too carried away, Candy. At these prices, I think I'll start out with the four-drawer model."

"Okay," she said with an accepting shrug. "Do you need anything else while we're here? Staples, pens, paper clips, notepads, message—oh, Nick! Look at that chair."

Before Nick could stop her, Candace had hurried over to an office display near the front of the store. Beneath an eight-foot-long executive desk of polished, inlaid teak, sat a high-backed swivel chair upholstered in butter-soft burgundy leather. She sat down in it and leaned back, letting it rock her weight for a time, and then turning it from side to side, listening for squeaks. She smiled when she heard none.

"It's magnificent, and so comfortable."

"I'm sure," Nick said, ambling up beside her.

"Just the thing an executive needs. You want to try it out?"

"No, thank you. I'm not in the market for a new desk and chair yet, just file cabinets. Maybe when I've gotten a few more accounts and can afford to relocate to one of the skyscrapers downtown, but not now."

Slowly, Candace got out of the chair. "Oh, yeah, that's right. I forgot. You *are* working under something of a handicap, aren't you?"

"Unfortunately. It's called very little money." But not for much longer. At the rate he was going, he would be moving up, literally, very soon.

"Well," she said, running her hand across the surface of the desk, "it doesn't hurt to plan ahead. You know, for the future."

That's exactly what I'm doing, Nick thought. Making plans for the future. Our future together. The trouble, he knew, was getting that point across to her. She could be so sweet and amenable when she wanted to be, like now, for instance. But there were times when she could be damnably hardheaded.

He glanced at his watch, breathing a sigh of relief when he saw that he still had a few hours left. He would need that much time and more to put his plan into action. Where it would go, he didn't yet know, but he had kept his distance from her all day long, just as he had promised. He hadn't touched her and he hadn't tried to come on to her. But once they were alone at his house, all the promises that he had made to her earlier would be null and void.

"You sure I can't interest you in any paper clips or staples?"

Nick laughed. "What is this? First you talk me into getting the bigger file cabinet and then you try to interest me in buying expensive furniture. Are you helping them out here on a commission basis or something?"

"No, I just thought that since we're already here we'd get some other things you might need. Little stuff, you know? If nothing else, it would certainly save you having to come back later on."

"Thanks for your concern, but I think the file cabinet is all I'm going to need."

Once he had paid for the file cabinet and made arrangements for the store to deliver it to his house, Nick ushered Candace out to the parking lot.

"So, what's next on your agenda?" she asked as he helped her into his truck.

"Oh, I don't know," he lied with an easy shrug. "What do you want to do?"

Candace glanced at her watch. "Well, it is getting kind of close to dinnertime."

"Are you hungry?"

"After that lunch we had? No, not particularly."

"Then what do you say we head back to my place for a while."

Though he had made the suggestion quite casually, with no hint of mischief in his tone, Candace couldn't avoid feeling a niggling of apprehension crawl up her spine. Alone with him, at his house? What was he up to?

"Your place?" she asked.

"Yeah."

"Nick . . ."

"You can help me pick out a spot in my office for the new file cabinet."

With an inner sigh of relief, Candace felt some of her apprehension fade.

"And then afterward," Nick said, "we'll go eat, if you feel like it. Does that sound okay?"

"It sounds fine to me."

Moving his furniture, Candace could handle. Anything else, though . . .

ℰ♥ 10

NICK'S HOUSE CAME AS A SURPRISE TO
Candace. From what little he had told her about it, she
expected to find it tiny and cramped, his advertising
paraphernalia stacked to the ceiling in every room. Instead, she found the house quite neat and tidy, a little
like Nick himself.

Standing beside him on his front porch as he wrestled
in the dim light of early evening to get his key into the
lock, she looked around, noting the slightly overgrown
hedges, the lawn that would soon need cutting, and the
decorative wrought-iron bars on the windows; a deterrent
to burglars but something of a safety hazard for anyone
inside if the house should catch on fire. Nevertheless,
the bars did blend well with the house's stucco exterior,
giving it something of a Moorish look.

His front door opened directly into the living room,
furnished in what Nick probably considered the absolute
essentials for a bachelor—a long couch with tables sitting
at either end, a long coffee table in front of it, a couple

of chairs strategically placed against one wall, and running along thc wall opposite the couch, a set of shelves that held a color TV and stereo components.

She followed him across the highly polished hardwood floor that lacked even the simplest of rugs, beneath an archway, and into his rather small dining room. Nick pushed through a pair of swinging doors that squeaked, and Candace found herself in his kitchen.

"Don't say it," he said. "I already know what you're thinking. Julia Child and Jeff Smith wouldn't be caught dead cooking a meal in a place like this."

Candace had to agree, although she had been thinking more of local celebrity chefs, like Steven Piles and Dean Fearing, instead of Jeff and Julia. Nick's cabinets, which she suspected numbered in the dozens, must have once been a bright turquoise, but now they were faded to a sad dingy blue green. The countertops had definitely seen better days, too; they were chipped and buckled in places, revealing dark, ugly stained wood beneath. And the appliances, all in sixties copper tone, looked as though they might have come from an elderly couple's garage sale.

"Does everything here work the way it should?" she asked, inconspicuously running her fingertips over the counter near the sink and coming away with a clean hand. Impressive, she decided. A clean bachelor.

"Oddly enough, they do."

"Then I don't think you have anything to complain about. The kitchen in my apartment isn't half this big, but it's big enough for what I need. The size of this place, I imagine you sometimes get lost." She realized that he could put a table large enough to seat eight in the middle of the floor, and he would still have plenty of room to walk around.

"No, that's never happened, not for the amount of

cooking I've done. See, I'm your actual fast-food junkie. Oh, I occasionally cook, but usually, if it doesn't come in a paper bag or a Styrofoam carton, I try to avoid it.''

Candace stared at him in disbelief for a moment and then chuckled. ''Sure, you do. And I suppose the next thing you'll be telling me is that the lunch we had today came from a drive-through window.''

''No, I won't. If you want to know the truth, it came from the deli section of our friendly neighborhood su-permarket.''

''That yummy fresh pasta salad?''

''Yep.''

''And the ham-and-cheese rolls?''

''Well, no. I made those myself. I sort of got the recipe on how to make them from my mom. But I did get all the stuff at the supermarket.''

Her blue eyes widened in surprise. ''I didn't know our supermarket sold prosciutto.''

Nick grinned as he stuffed the leftovers of their picnic lunch into his refrigerator. ''It does. See, the trick is that you've got to know the head deli man.''

''Do you? Know him, I mean.''

''I do now.''

''Gosh, I can't believe he made the prosciutto for you.''

''He didn't. He just had it hidden in his meat locker. Actually, good prosciutto, the kind that's imported from Italy, takes months and a lot of love to make. You've got to know how to cure it just right, what kind of sea-sonings go onto it, and the proper amounts, and how long to let it hang so it will dry out properly. Johnny just sliced it up for me. After, of course, he found out I was a fellow *Italiano*.''

''Our butcher is Italian?''

"Yeah, he sure is."

"From Dallas?"

"Nah, he's originally from south Philadelphia. Or was it Newark? I forget. Anyway, he moved down here a few years ago with his wife and kids. He told me he loves the winters here, but the summers he can do without."

Though she felt dumbstruck by the fact that Nick had unearthed so much information from a comparative stranger who had only said, "May I help you?" and "Thanks, come back again," Candace managed to find her tongue. "And you found out this man's life story by just ordering a pound of prosciutto from him?"

"Yeah."

Amazing, she thought. And then it hit her, and she wished she could kick herself. "You think you're so smart."

"What? What'd I do?"

"It was your accent the butcher recognized, wasn't it?"

Nick blinked in confusion. "What accent?"

"The one you're speaking with now."

He chuckled. "I don't have an accent."

"Yes, you do."

"Candy, honey, if anyone has an accent, it's you."

"Me?"

"Yeah."

She grunted in exasperation. "Wait a dog-gone minute. I'm a native. I was born and raised here. I don't have an accent."

"Well, you sure don't sound like me."

"No, I sound like *me*. Like a Texan. I never heard anyone say 'whaddayah,' and 'yoose guys' before, until I met you and Tony."

"You never did, huh?"

"No, I didn't."

"Uh-huh," he said, slowly nodding. "Well, it just might interest you to know that where I come from, everybody talks that way."

"There it is again."

"There what is?"

"Your accent. 'Tawks.' The word, Nick, is talks."

"Tokks?"

Candace couldn't stop herself from smiling, amused not only by his very feeble attempt to speak like a Texan but by the exaggerated movement of his jaw.

"Hey, don't laugh," he said, stepping closer to her. "I'm still new at this, remember? Give me a couple more months, a little more exposure to the natives down here, and I'll be saying 'y'all' with the best of them."

In Candace's opinion his "y'all" sounded more like "yowell," or the cry an alley cat in heat would make. She burst out laughing as he moved even closer to her, and to keep him away she elbowed him in the ribs.

"Stop it. Cut it out, Nick. That's the poorest excuse for a Texas accent that I've ever heard. No matter how hard you try, you know that you'll never be able to speak like a native. Never in a million years."

At the sight of the rosy blooms in her cheeks, the way her blue eyes glittered with merriment, Nick felt his humor begin to fade, another emotion replacing it almost immediately. "Wanna bet?"

"No, I don't want to bet." She hesitated a moment, trying to collect herself and praying that her amusement would dissipate. She had to remain cool, calm, sober, and on her toes at all times while around Nick. "But on second thought, maybe I should. This would be a sure thing. I'd win, hands down."

And then she glanced up at Nick and saw the warmth in his dark brown eyes. The warmth, the tenderness, the concern, the—oh, God, the love those two fathomless orbs possessed almost took her breath away.

"What do you say we give it a couple of decades before we shell out any hard-earned cash?" he said quietly.

As his deep voice washed over her like a heavy velvet cloak, she felt the mood between them change, become what she had desperately wanted to avoid.

"Nick . . . don't."

"Don't what, Candy?"

"*You* know."

"No, I don't. I can't read your mind. You're going to have to spell it out for me."

"All right, I will. You promised me last night, when I was stupid enough to agree to come with you today, that you wouldn't do this to me."

"Did I?"

"Yes."

"Are you sure?"

"I'm positive."

He shook his head. "I seem to recall a little different agreement. True, I did promise not to touch you or come on to you, and except for the couple of times I brushed against you—which were purely accidental, mind you— I've kept my word."

"You also promised you wouldn't bring up that night."

Oh, thank you, sweetheart, Nick's mind shouted. Thank you, thank you, thank you!

He had been waiting all day long for her to bring up the subject of the night they had spent together, the night that had changed his life. Hers too, even though he doubted she would admit it. But now that she had broached the subject, he wasn't about to let it slide. He was going to hang on to it, make her talk about it, until they had settled it between them. Even if they had to spend all of tonight doing it.

"What night?" he asked, knowing that if he continued to play ignorant, she would be forced to explain.

"*That* night, Nick. The night we—" Candace broke off, feeling tight knots forming in the pit of her stomach. She couldn't verbalize what had happened, what she had experienced with him, not to mention the hell she had suffered afterward. She wouldn't. In the long run, it wouldn't solve anything or change the past. It would only increase the unidentifiable thing that now vibrated so tangibly between them, make it all that much harder to control.

"The night we made love," Nick said. "Isn't that what you were going to say?"

"All right, yes!" Suddenly feeling as if the walls of the kitchen and Nick himself were closing in on her, Candace started retreating backward. "And now that I've said it, I think I'd better go home."

For each step of withdrawal that Candace took, Nick advanced one. "Why?"

"You know why."

"No, I don't. Tell me."

"Because it was wrong. Damn it, Nick, what we did that night was wrong, and we both know it."

"No, baby, I don't know any such thing. You see, I don't think it was wrong at all. What we shared couldn't possibly be wrong. It was beautiful."

"Stop it!"

"*You* were beautiful. I told you that then, and I'm telling you now."

Candace felt he was getting too close, too close to her and too close to repeating what he had said that night. "Stop it! I don't care what you tell me. I know for a fact that we never should have done it."

"But we did do it, and there's nothing that you or I can say or do now that will change that fact. Face it, Candy. It happened."

"Yes, I know it happened."

"And even though I doubt you'll admit it, you know that it was the most beautiful thing that either of us has ever experienced."

Their lovemaking, she realized, had been beautiful, but she still couldn't agree with him.

"You don't understand," she said, her voice soft and filled with remorse. "Until that night, I'd never . . ." Her words trailed off into nothingness, uncertainty slowly eating away at the apprehension building inside of her.

"I know." Nick ached to reach out to her, to pull her close to him and hold her, to absorb her fears and misgivings. But he knew he didn't dare. He couldn't—yet. If he touched her now, she would freeze up on him, deny everything, and try to run away. Her tenderness, her love for him would come only when she would allow it, and not before. "That's what made it so special. I may not have been your first, and God knows you weren't mine, but I know I was your most memorable."

The look of surprise in her eyes had him instantly backpedaling, groping for a reasonable explanation. "I'm not just saying that out of some overinflated sense of conceit, either. What we did *was* memorable for you. If it hadn't been, you wouldn't be fighting me so damn hard now."

"I'm not fighting you." Candace turned sharply and headed back into the living room.

"Then stop running away."

"I'm not running. I—I just think it's time I went home. It's getting late, and I've got to go to work tomorrow."

"Stop it, Candy. Stop coming up with these lame, feeble excuses. They're not doing either of us any good, and they're only making it harder."

"They're not lame or excuses. I really do need to get home, Nick."

"It's not even six o'clock yet. You've still got hours before you have to go to bed."

At his mention of the word "bed," Candace grew very still. The whole day had all been leading up to this one moment, she realized. Their shopping trip to Olla Podrida, where Nick had bought his new bed; their quiet, very pleasant picnic lunch at the Arboretum; his bringing her back here to his house so she could help him find a space for his new file cabinet . . . All of it had been designed for this one moment in time.

When she spoke, her words came out just above a whisper. "No matter what you say, I won't do it, you know."

"Won't do what?"

"Go to bed with you." She had done it once before and somehow had managed to live with the guilt, but she didn't think she could do it again. Once with Nick Giulianni was enough to last her a lifetime. It would have to be enough, because she couldn't risk a second time.

"Correct me if I'm wrong," Nick said, "but I don't recall any time within the last few minutes, or during the whole day for that matter, that I've asked you to go to bed with me."

"No, you haven't . . . yet."

"Is that what all this is about? You think I'm going

to ask you?'' He watched as she slowly turned her head, glancing over her shoulder at him. He not only saw the trepidation in her eyes, but he felt it radiating out to him like a heavy, consistent pulse beat. She looked so scared, so uncertain, he had to wonder if he had pushed her too far.

''I know you will,'' she said.

''No, I won't. I want to, yes, more than anything I've ever wanted in my life. But I won't. That move has to come from you this time, sweetheart.'' Slowly, he lifted a hand and let the fingers sift through her shoulder-length hair. ''Are you going to ask me?''

The seconds that passed between them seemed more like hours to Candace as she hesitated, wanting him so badly that she ached inside, yet knowing she couldn't have him, that she shouldn't have him.

Finally, she inhaled a deep breath. ''No, I'm not, Nick. I can't. I belong to Don.''

His fingers grew still. ''You do, huh?''

''Yes.''

''Does he know that?''

Puzzled, she blinked. ''What?''

''You heard me. Does Don know that you belong to him?''

''Well, of course, he knows. We've been seeing each other for over two years. I wouldn't dream of going with a man that long if I didn't think he—''

''Look, just forget him a minute, okay? What about you? What are you getting out of this?''

''What do you mean?''

''I mean, it all seems pretty one-sided to me. You're saying that you're his, but if I asked him, would he say that he's yours?''

Candace, unable to answer, merely swallowed.

"I hate to disillusion you, sweetheart, but there's two sides to every relationship, with both parties doing an equal amount of giving and taking. But from what I've seen of yours and Don's, he's the only one who's getting anything out of it. You're always there waiting for him, whenever he wants you. The question is, is he ever there for you when you need him?"

"Not always, no," she answered quietly. "He can't be. With his job, he has to travel a lot. You know that."

Nick heaved a sigh and let his hand drop from her shoulder. "When are you going to wake up and face the fact that your guy Don does a lot more than just travel?"

"I don't have to wake up, Nick. I already know it. He works, too."

"No, you don't understand what I'm saying. While you're stuck here at home twenty-four hours a day, seven days a week, waiting for him to breeze through town, he's out there on the road, living."

Only then did Candace realize what Nick was getting at. The very idea that he might be right, that he had voiced thoughts that she herself had had on more than one occasion, made the tense knots in her stomach even tighter. "Are you suggesting that Don's got another woman?"

"No, honey, I didn't suggest it—you did. Admit it, the possibility has crossed your mind, hasn't it?"

She squared her shoulders, feeling the need to defend Don and herself. "Maybe he has. But it doesn't really matter."

"It should matter."

"Well, it doesn't. I trust Don. I know you may find that hard to believe, but I do. Furthermore, I'm sure he trusts me."

"Trusts you? Yeah, you bet he trusts you. And you

want to know why? Because you're safe."

"Safe?"

"Yeah, safe."

"I don't know what you're talking about."

"Come on, Candy, you're intelligent, you can figure it out. You're always there for him, whenever he picks up the phone or drops by your apartment. You always look pretty for him, dress nicely, have your hair and face fixed. You make him feel good by catering to him. And you never make any demands on him."

"So, what's wrong with that?"

"Nothing, if some of the effort you put out for him is returned. Which, I suspect, it isn't." He waited half a heartbeat for her to contradict his allegation. But when she just stood there, staring up at him with a look of dawning enlightenment in her wide blue eyes, he knew he was right.

But the knowledge that he had finally made her realize what Don had been doing to her for the past two years didn't make him feel very good. In fact, it hurt. He could sense her mounting pain and wished he could obliterate it, take back everything he'd just said. But he couldn't. He had chipped away at her shell of self-delusion, and now that he had finally broken through it, he had to go on. In the end he might come to hate himself even more, but he didn't dare stop. He was too close to getting her to admit the actual truth.

"What's even worse, Candy, the only reason you keep hanging on to Don is because he's safe for you."

The lump in her throat made her sound hoarse. "You're wrong."

"No, baby, I'm right. He's safe. He doesn't make many demands on you, because he's never around. He's always out of town on a business trip someplace. But on the few occasions when he is in town, when he's with you and you're doing your best to please him, I'll bet he's not as grateful as you'd like him to be. In fact, it's my guess that he probably criticizes you. Does he? Does he always let you know that your way is wrong and his way is right?''

Candace lowered her head, unable to look at Nick any longer. ''I'm not perfect.''

''Not perfect? Oh, God, honey, nobody is. Don't you realize that? We're all human beings, and human beings are the most imperfect creatures on earth. That's what makes us all so unique, so special. And you're the most special person I've ever had the joyous pleasure of meeting. But you don't know that, do you?''

Slowly, he reached out to her, his finger lifting her chin so that she had to look at him. The sadness he saw in her eyes sent a knife blade slicing through his gut. ''Of course, you don't. You've been browbeaten for so long into believing that you had to be perfect, you've forgotten just how wonderful it is to be imperfect, just normal. Who did it to you, Candy? Who hurt you so badly?''

She wrenched her face away from his hand. ''No one. Don't talk nonsense.''

''It's not nonsense. Come on, tell me. Who did it?'' He paused, dreading having to ask the next question. ''Was it your father, when he left your mother?''

''*No!*''

Candace's vehement shriek echoed throughout the kitchen, telling Nick all that he needed to know. ''Oh, baby, it wasn't your fault. It wasn't your father's, either. Or your mother's. It wasn't anyone's fault. Marriages go bad, don't you know that?''

''Mine won't,'' she said defiantly.

"I know, because you don't ever intend to get married, do you?"

"Not ever get—that's the most ridiculous thing I've ever heard. Of course, I'm going to get married. Don and I—"

"No, you and Don won't!"

Nick's outburst caught Candace by surprise.

He took a deep breath, trying to bank down his mounting irritation. "Get this straight, Candy," he said. "Don hasn't asked you to marry him, and he never will, because he doesn't love you. You don't love him, either. You know it, and I know it. That's why he's so safe for you. Deep in your heart, or your subconscious, or wherever the hell else it counts, you know that he's not the marrying kind. That's why you've been sticking with him all these years. And that's why you're fighting me so hard now."

"Stop it, Nick." Candace knew he was getting too close to the truth. Much too close. And it frightened her.

"No way, baby. I'm not going to stop it until you understand where I'm coming from. I want to marry you. You know that I do, and the thought of it scares you to death."

"Shut up!" She whirled around and stormed out of the kitchen, wanting only to get as far away from Nick as fast as her two feet would carry her. He was much too dangerous, much too threatening to the safe little world she had built for herself.

But Nick was too quick for her. He caught up with her in the middle of the living room, grabbing her arm and spinning her around.

"I told you that night—*our* night together, remember? It was right after we had made love and you were still wrapped in my arms. God, Candy, I could feel your heart beating in the same rhythm as mine, we were so close. I told you then that I was going to marry you. I didn't ask you, I told you. And what did you do? You could have said thanks, but no thanks, or some other trite phrase that would let me know where I stood. But you didn't do that. You took the coward's way out and ran away from me so fast that I had to leave New York and move down here to catch you."

"Why? No one asked you to."

"I know no one asked me to. I did it all on my own, because I wanted to. Because I wanted you."

Candace felt a tiny pain pierce her heart. "No, you don't. You don't want me, so stop wasting your breath. Stop telling me all these lies."

"They're not lies."

"Yes, they are. Don't you see, Nick? All this . . . manure your handing me—it won't do you any good. You don't mean it now, and you certainly didn't mean it that night. You were only handing me a line, thinking it was some sort of compensation for the fact that I gave you a good time."

He stared at her, his gaze full of disbelief and bewilderment. "Is that what you think?"

"It's what I know."

"Well, you're wrong, Candy. I meant every word I said, that night and right now. Every goddamn syllable. I'm not like the other people in your life, who have said they loved you and then turned around and walked out on you. Candace McFarren soon-to-be Giulianni, I want you. I love you."

Her chest rose and fell rapidly as she studied him through a haze of skepticism. One part of her wanted to laugh hysterically in his handsome face, but another part of her, the stronger part, wanted desperately to believe him. And because she wanted to believe him, she felt her fears, her apprehensions, and her misgivings begin to fade, allowing a more primitive, volatile sensation to gain control.

"That's too bad, Nick, because I don't want you."

The soft uncertainty in her voice had Nick fighting back a smile. He knew he had finally won.

"You're lying," he said. "You do want me. You're standing here, listening to me, and you're not running away. That alone tells me you want me so badly right now that it's eating you alive."

Her mouth suddenly dry, Candace licked her lips.

"I can see it written all over your face." Feeling a surge of heat sear through his loins, Nick slowly advanced toward her. "You're remembering that night we spent together, aren't you?"

Yes, I am, damn you, a voice cried out in Candace's mind.

"You're remembering how terrific it was between us, how easy and natural we were together."

Please, Nick, stop doing this to me, she thought. Look away and let me go.

"It can be that way again, Candy. You know it, and I know it. All you've got to do is say the word."

Finding herself mesmerized by the deep timbre of his voice, Candace was unaware of stepping closer to him. One moment he was a few feet away, and the next, only inches separated them. But while her body responded, her mind still rebelled. "I'm not going to bed with you."

"I know."

Nick opened his arms, took one step closer to her, and let them close around her. "But we are going to make love. You got that, Candy? We're not going to have sex or screw around. We're going to make love."

"Yes," she said, simply, finally accepting the inevitable.

"And you're not going to regret it like the last time. I know you won't, because I won't let you."

✆ 11

WEARILY, COURTNEY PARKED HER
BMW in the center of the double garage. Her shoulders
and back ached from having sat at her desk since she
had arrived at work at eight that morning, not even taking
a break for lunch. The fingers of her hands ached from
having logged so much time on her computer. Even her
eyes ached. She had had a bitch of day at the office and
wanted nothing more than to go into the house, throw
her body into a hot bubble bath, and perhaps, if she felt
really adventurous, drink some wine as she watched the
week's worth of *Remington Steele* reruns she had taped
on her VCR.

Her day may have been forgettable, but at least she
had accomplished something. Mr. Bryant was happy.
Poor old fellow, she thought. He had finally decided to
sell his company here in Dallas to a conglomerate out in
California. For her, the impending sale meant more than
wording the contract just right, slanting it in his favor.
It also meant having to clear her appointment calendar

for a week or more and tie up all her other loose ends so that she could fly out to San Francisco in a few weeks' time and finalize the deal. But the hefty legal fee she would soon bring in would be well worth the time and effort. She might even have enough, after taxes, to take that cruise around the Mediterranean and see the Greek islands, as she had long wanted and never had the time to do.

She walked around to her front door and unlocked it, expecting to have total peace and quiet greet her. Instead, she groaned when heard the phone begin ringing.

"Oh, please don't be the office. I just left there, for Pete's sake." She hurried down the hall, her three-inch-high heels muffled by the thick carpet as she took the short flight of steps two at a time to the upper level. Once inside her study, she tossed her purse and briefcase onto her desk and grabbed for the phone.

"Hello."

"Court?"

Despite the voice on the other end of the line sounding so muffled, she recognized it immediately. "Candy?"

"Oh, God, Court."

Hearing the emotional tremor in her friend's voice, Courtney quickly moved around the desk and fell into her chair. She knew she was about to hear some bad news, and bad news always had to be heard sitting down.

"What is it, Candy? Did something happen to Ellie and Tony?"

"No."

"Is it your mom or dad?"

"No."

Courtney frowned. If it wasn't Ellie, or Candace's mom or dad, what else could be the matter?

And then a terrifying thought struck her. Could Candace be pregnant? It had been months since Candace and Nick had been together, and she had sworn to Courtney that they had been very careful. But accidents could happen, even to those who took precautions.

No, it couldn't be that, Courtney decided, and she began racking her brain for some other tragedy that might have upset her friend.

"Candy, did you get fired?"

"Mmm-mmm."

"Was that a yes or a no?"

A shakily indrawn breath and then Candy said, "No, I didn't get fired."

"Then what's the matter?"

"Everything. All this time I felt so sure that I was in control, that I could handle the situation—any situation— but was I ever wrong."

"About what?"

"About me. About Nick." Candace expelled a heavy sigh. "There's no beating around the bush. After today, I'm definitely a lost cause."

"Candy, could you be a bit more specific? I'm having an awfully hard time translating your cryptic remarks."

"All right. If you must know, it happened again."

It had to involve Nick, Courtney assumed, willing her blood pressure to calm down, drop lower, de-escalate . . . whatever blood pressure was supposed to do. But as she grew calmer the lawyer in her needed to hear Candace confirm her assumption, set her own mind at rest. "What happened again?"

"Nick and I. We—oh, God, Court!"

"It's all right, Candy. Just settle down. Things like this happen all the time."

"Not to me, they don't."

"Yeah, even to you, kiddo. You get around a good-looking guy like Nick Giulianni, your old hormones are bound to get a little screwy and go out of control.''

Candace snorted dryly. ''Is that your way of telling me that yours did when you were with him?''

''With whom—Nick?''

''That's who we're talking about, isn't it?''

''No, certainly they didn't. Why would they? I don't think of him in that way. But I've already told you that. To me, Nick is nothing more than a friend, a buddy, a— I don't know—a slightly older brother.''

''I wish I could think of him that way.''

Not in a million years, Courtney thought. You love him too much. And in spite of the hard time you've given him, he loves you.

But Candace was too stubborn to admit it. If she ever could, though, Courtney knew three lives would be made a lot simpler—hers, Candace's, and Nick's. But giving advice to the lovelorn was a job more suitable for Ann Landers, not an attorney who was accustomed to handling impersonal corporate mergers.

''I don't know why I keep torturing myself by doing this,'' Candace said.

''You mean, going to bed with him?''

''We did not go to bed, Court.''

Candace's firm tone told Courtney that her friend's earlier distress was at an end. And for that, she was grateful. She could talk to Candace, reason with her, when she was calm. Although why she wanted to bother, she didn't know. After the day she had just put in at the office, she wasn't sure she could handle any more crises successfully.

''Okay,'' she said, ''so you didn't go to bed with him. I'm sorry for jumping to the wrong conclusion.''

''You should be.''

"Look, Candy, I know you're upset right now, but if it's all the same to you, I'd rather not get into an argument with you, okay? I've had a day you would not believe. Can't you just accept my apology and leave it at that?"

"I don't know. You're always reading between the lines, assuming things that just aren't there."

"Well, what was I supposed to think? Good heavens, the phone's ringing off the wall as I walk in the door. And when I pick it up, it's you, weeping hysterically, telling me that *it* happened again. It's only natural I assume that *it* was you and Nick and a bed."

"Well, it wasn't. This time we—" Candace broke off, inhaling a ragged breath.

"This time you what?"

"This time we didn't even make it to the bed."

"You didn't?" Courtney couldn't help her smile of surprise. Sweet little Candy was beginning to loosen up, become more daring.

"No, we didn't."

"Then if a bed isn't in the picture, is it safe for me to assume that it was you and Nick and a couch?"

"No, not a couch, either. It was the floor. Oh, God, Court, why does this keep happening to me? I don't want it to happen, but it does."

It's called chemistry, kid, Courtney thought. That devilish old chemistry that makes idiots out of most of us at one time or another. You can't keep your hands off of him, and heaven knows, he can't keep his hands off of you.

"The question is," Courtney said, "are you sorry?"

"No. I mean, yes! Of course I'm sorry."

"No, I don't think you are."

"I am! Really, I am. I know it shouldn't have happened again. I certainly didn't plan for it to, but now

that it has, I've got to figure out a way to make sure that
history doesn't repeat itself anymore.''

''Why even bother?''

''Because it isn't right.''

''Who says?''

Courtney waited for a moment for Candace to answer,
but she only heard silence on the other end of the line.
A tired smile touched her lips. Congratulations, Nick,
she thought. It looks like you're finally making some
headway.

''I do,'' Candace said. ''I say it isn't right. If Don
ever found out what I've done, he would be crushed.''

Courtney couldn't suppress her snicker of amusement.
''Yeah, sure he would.''

''He would!''

''I don't think so. But why don't you try telling him
and find out for yourself, see if I'm not right.''

''Tell him? Do you know what you're suggesting?''

''Yeah, I sure do. I'm suggesting that you go over to
his apartment right now. Don't call him first. Just go on
over there—you might luck out and find him at home.
Tell him what's happened, make a clean breast of the
whole thing.''

''And risk destroying everything we've spent the last
two years building?''

''You mean, what *you've* spent the last two years
building, Candy. You've done all the work. Don hasn't
done a damn thing for your relationship that I can see.''

''Don't talk about him like that. He's a nice guy.''

''Maybe he is. I don't know him that well, I'll have
to take your word for it. But you've got to admit that,
nice aside, he's kind of dull, too.''

''Don, dull?''

''Yes, Don's dull. At Ellie and Tony's wedding all he

did was stand around, looking like some department-store mannequin. If he hadn't blinked and shifted his weight from one leg to the other occasionally, somebody would have carted him off to a storeroom. The whole time we were there, I didn't once see him dance or try to socialize with anyone other than—''

"Because he didn't know any of the other guests, that's why."

"He knew Ellie and me," Courtney said.

"Well, he spoke to you. Her too. I was right behind him in the reception line. I saw and heard him do it."

"And that was the end of his socializing, wasn't it?"

Candace paused, then said, "Some people are uncomfortable around large crowds of strangers. Don happens to be one of them."

"Face it, Candy, people in general make him uncomfortable." How Don had ever gotten into sales was a mystery to Courtney. In her opinion, he would have been better suited to frequenting quiet, confined places, like a public library. He never talked, never had any interesting anecdotes to tell, and if he had a personal history, it was probably as uninteresting as he was.

"Look, I don't want to talk about Don," Courtney said. "I don't think you want to talk about him, either, do you?"

"Yes, I do." Candace exhaled a long breath. "And as much as I hate to admit it, I think you might be right."

"About what?"

"About going over to his place and telling him what I've done."

Courtney pulled the phone away from her ear and stared at it in utter disbelief. Candace was going to take her advice? Amazing! She would have to remember to circle the date in red ink on her calendar so she could celebrate it occasionally. Chances were, this would probably never happen again.

"I think that's a very wise decision, Candy."

"I don't know how wise it is, but I've got to do it. If I don't, I won't be able to live with myself."

"Don't let this upset you," Courtney said. "If nothing else, telling Don will help to ease your conscience. You never know, it might even stop you from worrying so much. All the guilt you've been suffering lately isn't good for you. At the rate you've been going, you're going to have ulcers before you're thirty." *I know,* she added silently, *because living with you and your blasted puritanical scruples for the past twenty-two years have almost given them to me.*

"You're right. It's not good for me. It's not good for anyone. I think I'll try calling him first."

"Well, that's entirely up to you. If it were me, though, I'd just drive on over there. Even if he isn't at home, getting away from your apartment for a while will do you some good. You know, you really do need to get out more often."

Candace issued a mirthless laugh. "Jeez, Court, if you only knew. I've been out all day long."

"I said 'out.' That doesn't have a thing to do with going to and from work."

"That's what I just said. I didn't go to work today."

"You didn't?"

"No."

"Well, aside from doing the carpet lambada with Nick, what did you do?"

"Nothing much, really. I just helped him buy a bed and a file cabinet."

Just a bed and a file cabinet? Courtney shook her head in disbelief.

"And in between," Candace said, "we had a picnic lunch out at the Arboretum."

"No offense, Candy, but there are times when I honestly don't understand you. You claim not to like Nick. You've said over and over again that you have no feelings at all for him, other than occasional surges of uncontrollable lust. You suffer all kinds of hell after you've been with him. Yet you take a day off from work to help him pick out furniture and have lunch together in one of the most beautiful gardens in Dallas? I just don't get it."

"I never said I didn't like him."

"Then should I take that to mean that you do?"

A thoughtful silence filled Courtney's ear for a moment.

"Yeah," Candace said, "I suppose I do mean that."

"Let me take it one step further. Could you perhaps be in love with him a little bit?"

Another pause and then a ragged breath. "Oh, God, Court. I'm not sure, but I think I am."

"Then for heaven's sake, Candy, get rid of Don, go to Nick, and try to get on with your life."

"You mean, just dump him? Forget all the time we've spent together, what we've meant to each other, and just dump him?"

"Yeah. Trust me, kiddo, it's for the best."

Candace pulled into the vacant parking place directly in front of Don's apartment. The car next to hers, she saw, was Don's. She didn't cut the engine, but continued to let it run. Now that she knew he was at home and not still away on another of his endless business trips, she had to make a final decision about how to broach the subject with him.

All the way over to his place, she had tried to decide.

She had come up with one or two likely possibilities, but despite these, she still found herself in a quandary. Don didn't like people who skirted around issues for the sake of politeness; he liked them to get directly to the point. But she couldn't come right out and tell him what she had done with Nick. She might not love him as much as she once had, but that didn't mean she wanted to hurt him. And if she did just blurt out the truth, she would surely end up embarrassing herself.

"Best approach it slowly," she muttered as she turned off the ignition and climbed out of her car.

Yeah, that was what she would do. She would lead into the issue gradually, first asking him how his trip went, and then she would move to more sensitive specifics.

Don's apartment, like all of the others in the complex, was a two-story studio—two bedrooms and a bath upstairs; living room, dining room, kitchen, and half bath downstairs. His front door, bearing its own mail slot, was protected by a slight overhang supported by two brick columns. Candace walked toward the door hesitantly, climbing the two steps to his minuscule porch more like an elderly disabled person rather than a twenty-seven-year-old woman.

Give me strength, she prayed, lifting a hand and depressing the button on the doorbell. Help me get through this without hurting him, please.

Before she could finish the plea to her higher authority, the door opened.

Don blinked, surprised to see her, then a pleased grin split across his face. "Candy!"

"Hi."

He stepped out onto the landing and wrapped his arms around her, making her feel more guilty than protected.

"What are you doing here?"

"I, er . . ."

"Tell me later. Come on in. I just got home myself a couple of hours ago. I had a bitch of a flight in from Phoenix, let me tell you. We caught air pockets all the way. And the traffic coming in from the airport—it was unbelievable. I swear, LBJ is getting about as bad as Central Expressway this time of day. But it's the last rush-hour traffic jam I'll have to suffer through for a while, thank God."

As he spoke she glanced around his living room. If he had been home for a couple of hours, why were his bags still sitting beside the front door? Why hadn't he taken them upstairs to his bedroom and unpacked them? Normally, Don wasn't a lazy man; he liked to do things right away, get them over and done with. But it looked to Candace as though he might be getting ready to leave again.

She looked pointedly at the bags and then at him. "Are you taking another trip?"

"You bet I am," he said with a wide grin. "I'm leaving tomorrow night."

"But I thought you just said you were going to be home for a while."

"No, I said I wouldn't have to suffer through traffic jams for a while. And I won't. There's no business involved on the trip I'm taking this time. It's purely for pleasure. I'm taking a long overdue vacation. Well, it's not a vacation in the literal sense. I'm going to Florida to visit my folks."

"Your folks, huh?"

"Yeah. I decided it was high time I saw for myself how they were getting along. And with all the traveling I've done for the past few years, this trip's going to be a freebie. You wouldn't believe the number of frequent-flier miles I've racked up.''

Yes, Candace would. Considering that he had been gone from home five days out of seven since she had first known him, he could probably make a couple of round trips to the moon and still have lots of mileage left over.

''Well, it's going to be a freebie as far as the plane fare is concerned,'' he said. ''I figured while I was in Orlando, I'd get in a little sight-seeing. You know, take my sister's kids to Disney World and places like that. That'll run into some bucks, I'm sure, but I'm not going to sweat it. I figure I deserve this break.''

But what about me? a voice cried out in Candace's head. If she hadn't dropped by, would he have bothered to call her and tell her of his plans? Or would he have just ignored her, as he'd done so often in the past?

Probably the latter, she decided, feeling an odd elation at his remarks.

Elation? That shocking awareness brought her up short. How could she feel elated when the man she thought she loved had just informed her that he was leaving town again, that he wouldn't be spending any of his vacation time with her? By all rights, she should be distressed at the notion.

Though confused at her own conflicting emotions, she had to admit that the knowledge somehow managed to eliminate a lot of the guilt that she had borne for so long. And the absence of that guilt seemed to clear her thoughts, give her direction and purpose. She realized that she couldn't beat around the bush with Don, that she had to come right out and confess everything to him. After all, she now knew she had nothing to lose.

''Don, there's something I have to tell you.''

"Sure, shoot," he said, sauntering toward his kitchen. "Want something to drink? I'm not sure what I've got, but I think there's a leftover soda in the fridge."

"No, thank you. I'm not thirsty."

Stopping just inside the kitchen doorway, Don turned. Only then did he finally noticed her serious expression. "Hey, what's the matter?"

Candace opened her mouth, ready to tell him everything, needing desperately to get it off her chest, but the right words just wouldn't come. Instead, she shook her head with a sigh and sat down on his couch. "Everything."

"Come on, Candy, it can't be that bad." He crossed toward her and sat down close beside her, covering her hand with one of his as the other arm wrapped around her shoulder.

At one time his touch, his nearness would have sent shivers of pleasure and enjoyment down her spine. Now she felt nothing but his body warmth, and it made her uneasy.

"But it is that bad," she said.

"Well, just tell old Uncle Don what's bothering you. I'm sure we can figure out something to do."

"*Uncle* Don?"

He laughed. "Well, it sounds a little better than Friend Don, don't you think? I don't know—friend's got too much of a religious ring to it."

Where the weight of worry and guilt had left Candace, a feeling of sadness now took its place. "Is that how you see us, as friends?"

"Yeah. You're about the best friend I've got."

"I'm nothing else to you?"

He studied her through a puzzled scowl. "Like what else would you be?"

Candace shook her head and slowly edged away from him. "After two years, I would have thought we'd be more than friends. A lot more."

His perplexity increased. "I don't know what you're getting at."

"You and me, Don. Two whole years of us working at being a couple. That's what I'm getting at."

"You think—" He broke off, a sudden enlightened look erasing the wrinkles of confusion on his forehead. "Of course, what else could you have thought. Jesus."

"I've been wrong, haven't I?" She couldn't hide the disappointment in her voice. "All this time, there never has been an us, has there? It's been me, and only me, believing that there was something between us."

"Hey, look, Candy, I—"

"No, it's all right, Don. *I'm* all right." She rose to her feet, intending to leave, her purpose in coming no longer relevant.

But Don reached out a hand and pulled her back down beside him. "The hell you are. I've hurt you. God knows I didn't mean to, but it's as plain as the nose on your face that I have."

"No, you haven't hurt me. This is all my fault, not yours. I may be disappointed and a little embarrassed, but I'm not hurt."

Don expelled a sigh of frustration as he shook his head. "All this time I thought you understood about us."

"I thought I did, too," she said. "I thought we were building a strong relationship, taking our time in getting to know one another before we took that big final step."

"You thought that?"

Despite the look of shock on his face, Candace nodded. It was better, she knew, to be brutally truthful with him than to let this farce go on any longer.

"Did I really give you that impression, lead you on like that?" he asked. "Because if I did, I'm sorry."

"No, you have nothing to be sorry for. Looking back on it now, you didn't do anything, Don. Like I said before, I'm to blame for everything. My own silly delusions about us and our so-called relationship. My belief that one day we would get engaged and then marry. I'm to blame for it all."

"I wish I had known what you were thinking. If I had, I might have been able to do something."

"Don't shortchange yourself. You did a lot. You were a very good friend. You still are. I see that now."

"Do you?"

"Yes. Believe me, I do."

"Because that's all I wanted from you, Candy. Friendship. Honest to God, that's all I wanted."

"I'll admit," he said, "that the idea of going to bed with you crossed my mind. To be perfectly honest, it crossed my mind a lot of times, but I knew it wouldn't be right, so I never pressed the issue. I couldn't. I just didn't have the heart. I suppose I was still too raw."

Now it was Candace's turn to look puzzled. "What do you mean?"

"Well, you know. When we first met and started going out together, I hadn't been divorced very long."

"Divorced?" Shock registered throughout her body and settled in her face.

"Yeah."

"You've been married?"

"Yeah, didn't you know?"

"No. You never told me. You never said one word."

"I'm sorry, I thought I had."

"Well, you didn't. We've dated for over two years and this is the first time I've heard anything about it.

Jeez, you think you know somebody and then this happens.'' She gave her head a brisk shake and glared at him. "Why were you keeping it such a secret?"

"I wasn't," he said. "At least, I hadn't thought I was until now."

"Divorced," Candace muttered, still trying to comprehend the fact that at one time he had had a wife. Possibly even—"Do you have any children that you've been keeping from me?"

"Yeah. My little girl, Suzie. But I wasn't trying to keep her a secret, either."

"Then why didn't you ever talk about her?"

"I don't know. I guess the subject of kids just never came up in our conversations."

"Why don't you have any pictures of her here in your apartment?" Oh, God, Candace thought, feeling anger bubble up inside of her. Don couldn't be ashamed of his own child, could he?

"Because I don't have any." Don's hollow voice lacked any trace of animation. "Her mother left me when Suzie was just a baby. She ran off with her and I don't know where they are. I don't even know what she looks like."

Candace's mounting rage died a sudden death. She now understood why he had never spoken about his past. It probably hurt him too much to remember. "Oh, Don, I'm so sorry. I didn't know."

"It's all right. Maybe if I had opened up to you and told you all this a long time ago, we wouldn't be sitting here now, having this conversation."

Oh, yes we would, Candace's conscience cried out, reminding her that she had yet to tell him about Nick. Despite the fact that she now knew her relationship with

Don had never been what she thought, he still had a right to know.

"The reason I came over here today wasn't to delve into your private secrets, your personal tragedies," she said.

"It wasn't?"

"No." She took a deep breath and let her conscience have its say. "I've met a man, Don."

"You have?" His face registered surprise and honest pleasure.

"Yeah."

"Do I know him?"

"I don't know. You've met him. He was at Tony and Elise's wedding. The tall guy with the black hair? Tony's best man."

"Oh, yeah! He was from New York, wasn't he?"

Candace nodded. "He's now living here in Dallas."

"No kidding?"

"Yes, no kidding."

"Did his job transfer him down here?"

"Not exactly."

Don paused a moment, then chuckled. "Are you saying that he moved down here because of you, to be near you?"

"Yes."

"I'll be damned. That's great, Candy!"

Candace smiled feebly, glad that he seemed so pleased. At least one of them felt good about this debacle; the verdict was still out as far as her feelings were concerned.

Don saw her lack of excitement and thought he recognized it as guilt. "Ah, now I see. I think I'm finally getting the picture."

"What picture?"

"You and this new guy of yours. And me too, I suppose. You came over here today thinking you were going to have to dump me, didn't you? That's why you came in looking so upset, why you look so upset now."

"Yes," she said. "I couldn't keep up with the pretenses any longer. Before I did anything else, I had to find out where I stood with you."

"And now that you know where we stand?

"I—" She broke off and shook her head slowly. "To be perfectly honest, Don, I'm still as confused as ever. I mean, I know now that you and I aren't what I thought we were, but that's still not enough."

Don nodded. "What about this other guy? Do you love him?"

Love? Candace knew that she and Nick certainly had a lot of chemistry going for them. Either chemistry, or plain old hormonal lust. But love, the actual till-death-do-us-part kind?

Love, she knew, could never be just one-sided. Both parties had to give and take it equally for a relationship to work. If it wasn't equal, the love could die a miserably prolonged death.

"Maybe," she said quietly. "Maybe not. I'm not sure yet."

"It seems to me that you were sure enough that it was to come over here and break up with me."

"But I didn't come over with the intentions of breaking up. I came over to find out once and for all just how you felt about me, if there was a chance for us. My God, we've spent the last two years together, Don. There hasn't been anyone else for me but you." She sighed. "I had a birthday the other day—my twenty-seventh. And while that's not exactly decrepit or near retirement age, I'm certainly not getting any younger."

"None of us are, Candy."

Hearing the solemn ring to his tone, she looked up and saw the sadness in his eyes. Until now, she hadn't known just how lonely Don was. Oh, sure, he traveled and saw different and sometimes exciting new places, but when he came home, it was always to an empty house. He had no wife, no children—he had no one, but himself. Himself and an occasional good friend.

Candace's heart swelled with tenderness. She reached up and wrapped her arms around Don's neck. "You'll find somebody one of these days. When you least expect it, she'll come waltzing into your life and change it forever."

"You think so?"

"I know so."

Don tightened their embrace. "I sure hope you're right, Candy. God knows, I hope you're right."

12

AN INTENSE PAIN SHOT ACROSS COURT-
ney's shoulders and up the back of her neck. To alleviate
the discomfort, she turned her gaze away from the
mounds of opened law books in front of her and slowly
straightened her back, moving her head carefully from
side to side until some of the pain dissipated. She had
known that getting Mr. Bryant the kind of deal he wanted
might take some sort of toll on her, but she hadn't figured
it would involve anything as excessively agonizing as
what she had just experienced.

"Taking a break?"

Courtney looked toward her office doorway and
blinked in surprise when she saw David Ballard standing
there. He leaned against the jamb, the coat to his suit
discarded, his black tie loosened at the collar, his shirt
sleeves rolled up to his elbows. The only indication of
whimsy about the man that she could see was his bright
red suspenders. They were a token gesture of rebellion,
she decided, to his usual austere legal garb.

"Yes, I'm taking a break," she said. "I think I deserve one, considering I've been at this contract for a good six hours."

"Need some help?"

"No, thank you. I'll get it . . . eventually. If I don't go blind first."

David pushed away from the doorway and started toward her, his long legs moving with an inherent rhythmical grace. "Got a neck ache?"

"A neck ache, a backache, a headache . . . you name it. I'm not sure, but I think I might be falling apart."

With a chuckle, David moved to stand behind her chair, his hands coming to rest on her shoulders, his thumbs digging gently into the tense muscles at the base of her neck.

Courtney's first reaction was one of shock. In the three years that she had worked for the law firm, she had never once known David to show this sort of intimacy with anyone in their office. Oh, sure, he would smile or laugh at a joke, or offer a frown of sympathy when one was called for, but nothing as personal as a neck massage.

But her shock vanished, and she dismissed all thoughts of David Ballard's always-so-proper office behavior when his warm, subtle touch penetrated the tension in her muscles, manipulating it and the pain she felt into oblivion. As she let him have his way with her, her head swayed to one side and a sigh of contentment escaped her lips.

"How does that feel?" he asked.

"Marvelous. Don't stop."

His hands slowly moved away from her neck, his fingers lowering to investigate the shape of her shoulders through the silkiness of her blouse.

"We're the only two left here in the office, you know."

Despite his soothing voice, his magnificent touch, the warmth spreading through Courtney ended abruptly. Her eyes opened wide. "We are?"

"Um-hmm."

"Where is everybody?"

"They've all gone home for the day."

She glanced at her wristwatch, but her eyes refused to focus on the tiny face. "What time is it?"

"Almost eight."

"Almost eight? Good heavens! I've been working on this for twelve hours, not six."

He patted her shoulders and moved back to stand in front of her desk. "When you start losing track of the time, it's a sure sign that you need to go home. Don't worry; this will all still be here waiting for you tomorrow morning. You can pick it up right where you left off."

"Good thinking." Courtney took a moment to mark the pages in the law books with bookmarks before she stacked them on the corner of her desk. "I don't mind telling you, I'll be happy when we get this whole Bryant-Silvatech merger settled and put behind us."

David cocked his head to one side in concern. "Is the business beginning to wear you out?"

"No, not at all. The business part is fine. It's this darn contract—making sure I've crossed all the *T*s and dotted all the *I*s. After all the trouble we've gone through for Mr. Bryant—what am I saying? After all *he's* been through, poor man, I would hate to have some little unseen glitch throw us right back to square one. I do not want to have to start this thing over again. One merger as complicated as this one is enough to last a lifetime, thank you very much."

David stood at the door, waiting for her to collect her purse and briefcase and slip on the coat to her suit.

"Look at it this way," he said, turning off the lights and closing the door behind them. "Come the first of next month, we can go to San Francisco and say good-bye to Mr. Bryant and Silvatech forever."

Courtney hadn't taken more than two steps out of her office when she came to a sudden stop in the hall. "We?"

"Mmm-hmm."

A gnawing suspicion began to form in the back of her mind, one that brought unsettling feelings with it. "You're going with me?"

Hearing the question in her voice, David chuckled and shook his head. "I know what you're thinking, Courtney, but you're wrong. I trust you. Don't think for a minute that I don't."

"Then why the sudden decision to go to San Francisco with me?"

"Because it's your first big deal." He looked down at her and saw the lingering look of doubt on her face. "I don't get a chance to have many thrills in my life these days. What with all my administrative duties here at the office and my heavy caseload, I do very little else but work. I want to be in 'Frisco to see you pull off this merger. If nothing else, it'll let me relive my first deal." A boyish grin split his face. "Believe it or not, I banked a whole five hundred dollars from it."

Only five hundred? Courtney thought in amazement. Her cut of the law firm's percentage from Bryant's merger could climb well into the six-figure bracket—if Silvatech agreed to their terms. Compared to that, five hundred seemed like peanuts. Who was she kidding? It was peanuts.

"I know it's not a lot now," David said. "To be

honest, it wasn't a lot ten years ago, but at the time it was the most money I had ever made.''

Courtney noted David's wistful smile as they advanced down the hall toward the firm's main reception area, and came to a surprising conclusion. ''You love all this, don't you? All this wheeling and dealing where millions, sometimes billions, are at stake?''

''It's what makes life interesting. Well, it makes *my* life interesting, anyway. I can't speak for any of the other senior partners.''

Courtney gave a grunt of disbelief. ''Am I hearing you correctly? You're saying that this office and your client list are all that you have? That it's everything?''

''Well, no, of course not. I do have my Porsche to worry about. Here of late, I'm always taking her into the shop with one kind of problem or another. I'm afraid the poor old girl's just about had it.''

''Wait a minute. What about your family?''

''My family consists of me and my mother, and she's off living the fun life in sunny south Texas.''

''Just you and your mom?''

''Yeah, just us two.''

''But I thought you had brothers and sisters and a whole herd of nieces and nephews.''

David threw back his head and laughed. ''I don't know where you heard that from, but you heard wrong. I'm an only child. You may be thinking of my godchildren. I've got two of them, but they're both grown and in college now. It's been years since I even got to toss the ball around with them or play a little one-on-one basketball.''

She cast him a studious sidelong glance as they drew close to the elevators. Perhaps he had no family to speak of, but she had no doubt that he certainly had women in his life. And where there were women, David couldn't be as lonely as he let on. If only half of the rumors that she had heard bandied around the office about him were true, then he definitely had quite a few women. Probably a small harem by the sound of it.

No, not probably, Courtney decided. Unquestionably. As handsome as David was, not to mention suave, sophisticated, and almost obscenely wealthy, he could have any woman he wanted, anytime he wanted.

Any way he wanted.

Realizing where her thoughts were headed, she brought herself up short. She had to stop thinking of David Ballard in terms of some sort of sex object, some sort of female fantasy of a knight in shining armor come to life. He was her boss, her mentor, so to speak, and nothing more.

The elevator doors opened and they stepped inside, David pushing the button that would take them to their cars, parked in the basement garage.

"How's your friend doing?" he asked.

Courtney hesitated. "Which one?"

"The one who got married earlier this year."

"Oh, Ellie! She's just fine." If he had been asking about Candace, Courtney wasn't sure how she would have answered him. She had learned over the years that for the most part, women's personal problems didn't interest men. So she knew that David wouldn't want to hear that poor Candace was still as confused as ever, not knowing what to do, or who to do it with.

"She moved to New York City, didn't she?"

"Yeah, the big bad Big Apple."

"How does she like it? Is everything going okay for her there?"

"Things couldn't be better, to hear her tell it."

"I can imagine it must have been something of a culture shock for her, having to move from Dallas to New York so soon after she was married."

"Yeah, you could say that. She told me that when she first got there, she was too afraid to even leave the apartment. She didn't go out for two whole weeks."

"I don't blame her," David said. "I've been to New York, and those streets at night are no safe place for a woman to be on her own. A man, either, for that matter."

"No, I'm not talking about just at night. She wouldn't leave the apartment during the daytime. But then her husband, Tony, took her in hand and made her go out. It must have loosened her up some, because now she goes all over the place. She's probably been to every museum and art gallery and department store in town by now."

"New York certainly has a lot of those," he said.

"I know."

"Oh, have you been there?"

"Once, quite a number of years ago." Courtney smiled wistfully. "My father took me there as a high-school graduation present. A lot of the other girls at school got cars or trips to Europe for graduation; I was given a grand tour of the Big Apple."

"Any particular reason, or was it just because you'd never been there and wanted to go?"

The chuckle Courtney issued held a faint note of self-derision. "You really want to know?"

"Yeah. Why, is something wrong?"

"No, it's just that looking back on it, I get very embarrassed at the reason why Daddy and I went." She cleared her throat and gave him a straightforward look. "When I was a teenager, I had a—burning desire, I guess you could call it—to be an actress."

David grinned. "Really?"

"Yeah, really. I had always had the lead in all our
school plays and spring musicals. I could sing and dance
and play the piano, so I was certain I was Broadway-
star material.''

"Did you try out for a part, go to—what do they call
them?—cattle calls.''

"One," she said. "I went to one.''

"And?''

"Well, needless to say, it was an eye-opening experience. All those people—men and women both—most
all of them years older than me, still trying to get their
foot in the door. And there I was, a naive little eighteen-
year-old girl from Dallas, Texas, with her daddy waiting
for her back in a hotel room, believing that she could be
the next Mary Martin or Carol Channing. Believing,
mind you, that she would take the New York theater
scene by storm.''

"Should I take that to mean you didn't get the part?''

"Are you kidding? I didn't even make the first cut.
The casting director took one look at me and said, 'Sorry,
kid, you're not the type we're looking for. Next!' ''

David winced in commiseration. "That must have
hurt?''

"Yeah. At the time it hurt a lot. But by the time I got
back to the hotel—I walked all twenty-five blocks, by
the way—I had convinced myself that Broadway wasn't
for me, that I could do a lot better.''

The elevator doors opened and they stepped out into
the darkened parking garage.

"I don't suppose you ever thought of turning your
sights on Hollywood, did you?''

"Nope. I figured that since I had given Broadway my
best shot and they didn't want me, that automatically let
Hollywood out of the picture, too.''

"So what did you do?"

"I listened to Daddy, took his advice, and enrolled in the University of Texas that fall. I got my degree in law, and I haven't looked back since."

"And you don't regret choosing law over the theater?"

Courtney's sudden outburst of laughter echoed off the walls of the stark concrete garage.

"What's so funny?"

"You, of all people, David, should know that law *is* the theater. We've got better actors in the bar association than they'll ever have in Actors Equity. Some of our so-called honored colleagues give superb Oscar-winning performances each time they go before the bench. And that includes you."

"Now, wait a minute . . ."

"Don't take that the wrong way. It's not an insult; it's a compliment. I've seen you in action a few times. I know."

"But I'm not acting when I'm in court. I'm doing my job, giving the best defense that I can for my client."

"You do a lot more than that. The way you grab hold of a jury, wrap them around your little finger—that most certainly is acting. The best type of acting around, in my opinion. You mesmerize everyone in the courtroom. No ordinary performer can do what you do, time and time again. You just never get to take curtain calls, that's all."

"Curtain calls, ha!" he said. "You don't get curtain calls for presenting the facts to a jury in the best way you know how."

"No, you just get a verdict in your client's favor almost every time."

"Well," he said, grinning slightly, "there's usually

a lot of money at stake. And you know what they always say about money.''

"Yeah, it talks.''

"Sometimes very loudly. The louder the better, in some instances.''

They started toward their cars, walking past the empty spaces, their loud footsteps sounding almost eerie.

"What made you decide to go into corporate law?'' Courtney asked.

"Criminal law.''

"Excuse me?''

"Criminal law made me go into corporate law. You see, before I joined Stanhope and Frazier—''

"Now Stanhope, Frazier, and Ballard,'' she said.

"Yeah, well, before then—long before then, I was a public defender.''

She stared up at him in amazement. "You?''

"Yes, me.''

"That's hard to believe, David.''

"Tell me about it. I find it hard to believe myself. But I was. I handled nothing but dregs. That's what we called all the hopeless, lost-cause cases.''

"No drug dealers, I hope.''

"Not me. I handled your basic impoverished citizens who were in desperate need of legal counsel. Some of the other guys in the office handled the pushers.''

"Well, that's a relief to know,'' she said. "So how long were you with the PD's office?''

"Two or three years.''

"And you came to Stanhope and Frazier straight from there?''

"Yeah. Frazier discovered me, so to speak.''

"How?''

"Oh, he came into the courtroom where I was defending a particularly difficult case. I suppose he liked what he saw and thought I had potential, because he made me an offer I couldn't refuse.''

Courtney smiled. ''You got your client off, I take it?''

''You could say that.''

The flatness of David's remark roused Courtney's curiosity. ''Was he guilty?''

''Yeah, guilty as sin. I'd been handling his case for a while. Nonpayment of child support.''

''Oh, no, not one of those.''

''Yeah, one of those. Only his situation was a little different from most of the others you hear about. He flat didn't have the money for his three kids. Kids he loved dearly, by the way—I could tell that from the very beginning.

''He'd been laid off from his job, evicted from his apartment, had his fifteen-year-old used car repossessed. . . . You name it. The poor man was about as low and depressed as you could get. But despite all his hardships, his ex-wife still insisted on pressing charges.''

They reached Courtney's car, and David stood there, staring off into space as she unlocked the door.

''What happened?'' Courtney asked, intrigued with his story.

''About a month before Frazier walked into the courtroom and discovered me, my client got hold of a bottle, got drunk—stinking drunk. Then, somehow, he got hold of a gun.''

Courtney didn't have to hear the rest of David's story to know what had happened, why he had been in court with his client the day Frazier walked in.

''He killed his ex-wife,'' David said. ''Shot her once, right through the heart. He would have turned the gun on himself, but the neighbors heard them fighting and called the police. The squad cars rolled up just in time to stop him from committing suicide.''

''Where is he now, in prison?'' Or had the state already executed him?

David laughed, a hollow mirthless sound. ''No, as a matter of fact, he and his three kids are living somewhere in east Texas.'' He turned to look at her. ''I got him off.''

''On what, temporary insanity?''

''Nope. Self-defense.''

''Self-defense? How? *He* had the gun. *He* threatened her. Hell, he used it on her.''

''I know. But I persuaded the jury to believe that he was the injured party. After all, his wife was the one who had walked out on him. She had taken his kids away from him and everything else he possessed. Even his self-esteem. He had one tiny shred of pride left, and he was determined not to let her take that away, too.

''Besides,'' David said, ''it was the first criminal act the man had ever committed. Criminal? It was his first illegal act, period. He'd never even had so much as a parking violation. He had always paid his rent, his taxes, his bills. . . . He was a good, decent man who, due to circumstances totally beyond his control, had reached the end of his rope. He could see no other way out.''

''And the jury acquitted him.''

''Yeah, they sure did. And as far as I know, he's kept his nose clean ever since.''

Courtney expelled a heavy sigh of utter disbelief.

''But because of that one case, my one 'dreg' that turned ugly, I've now got a cushy six-figure-a-year job and my name embossed on the firm's stationery. Not a pretty story, is it?''

''No, it certainly isn't,'' she said. ''But if I'd been in

your shoes, I suppose I would have done the same thing.''

"Of course you would have. I was the man's attorney. It was my job to give him the best defense I possibly could, and I did.''

He turned to face her, his uneasiness with his past victory fading somewhat. ''But enough about law. What are your plans for this evening?''

His question took Courtney by surprise. ''Plans?''

''Yeah. You were planning to have dinner tonight, weren't you?''

''Well, yes, of course I was.''

''Then how about having dinner with me?''

''You?''

David chuckled. ''I know it's hard to believe, but I do eat every now and then.'' He closed the few feet that separated them. ''Sometimes even with a member of the opposite sex. How about you?''

Courtney felt his nearness begin to do strange things to her heart, its normal rhythm increasing. ''How about me what?''

''Do you sometimes eat dinner with members of the opposite sex?''

''Yes. Sometimes.''

He lifted a hand and brushed a dark curl away from her forehead, his fingers carefully arranging it with the other strands of hair atop Courtney's head. ''You know, we're going to have to do something about this?''

Her hand flew up to her hair. She had been working for hours without a break and hadn't combed her hair or freshened her makeup since early that morning. Heaven only knew what she must look like. ''I'm probably a horrible sight.''

''I'm not talking about how you look, Courtney. You look beautiful. I'm talking about us.''

And then his hand lowered to her chin and tilted it so that she had to look up at him. In the dim light of the parking garage she saw warmth in his deep gray eyes. Warmth, weariness, and undisguised passion.

Then he dropped his mouth to hers and sipped from her lips with a gentleness that had her legs turning weak and unsupportive.

"But not now," he said, pulling away. "And not tonight. As much as I would like to whisk you off to a quiet little restaurant and ply you with wine for the next few hours, I can't. I have the need but not the energy. I'd probably fall asleep in my soup." His smile radiated fatigue. "Maybe some other time."

Dumbstruck by his kiss, by how she felt about being in his arms, Courtney could only nod.

"See you in the morning, Courtney."

She watched as he turned and walked away, his footsteps echoing off the bare concrete walls.

"Yeah, see ya," she mumbled, completely mystified by his actions.

ᕲᕱ 13

NICK PULLED UP INTO COURTNEY'S driveway, his headlights sweeping past the neatly pruned hedges, the darkened windows, and the even darker-looking front porch. He didn't pause to consider that Courtney might not be at home; he killed the engine of his pickup and leaped out of the cab, leaving his door open as he dashed around the back to the porch.

He rang the doorbell with nervous staccato jabs of his finger, praying for Courtney to appear quickly. When no one came, his frustration and worry increased. He began pounding on the thick wood frame, causing the one-of-a-kind leaded-glass pane to rattle ominously.

"Oh, for God's sake, Court, get down here and open up!"

At that moment a pair of bright headlights glinted off the door in front of him and he turned sharply. Courtney, he finally realized, had just come home.

He didn't wait for her to come to him. He jumped off the porch and hurried down the sidewalk to the driveway, where she sat inside her white BMW, waiting for the automatic garage door to finish opening.

"We got trouble," he said.

Courtney depressed a button in her car and her window rolled down with a classy hum. "I didn't hear you. What did you say?"

"I said, we got trouble. Candy's missing."

"Missing?"

"Yeah. I've been calling her all day, but she's not at her apartment and she didn't go to work."

"Wait a minute. Let me get this thing parked in the garage, and then we'll go inside and talk. But stop worrying. Chances are, she's all right."

"I hope to God you're right. I'm worried sick about her, Court."

Courtney could see that. Even with the absence of light, she could see that his normally ruddy complexion was a few shades paler. But Candace missing? She didn't believe it. Candace wouldn't do such a thing. Not voluntarily, at least. She had too much sense.

Once inside the house, Courtney headed toward the kitchen, turning on the lights as she went. Nick, trailing along in her wake, turned them off again.

"Are you sure she wasn't just out of the office, running some kind of errand for one of those screwball scientists of hers?"

"I'm positive. I talked to just about everybody there, from the personnel director on down to some woman by the name of Shelly."

"Shelly? Oh, yeah, I've heard Candy speak of her before. I think they used to work together in the same office or something until Candy got promoted up to R and D. If you can call that a promotion. But Shelly hasn't seen or heard from Candy, either?"

"No. All she could tell me was that somebody named Dr. Franklin was climbing the walls. Mad as hell, too, according to Shelly."

"About what?"

"You'd better sit down for this one."

Courtney didn't like the tone of Nick's voice; it sounded too ominous. Now inside the kitchen, she ignored the need to get herself something to eat and drink, to stave off starvation. Instead, she pulled the kitchen stool away from the bar and sat down.

"Go ahead," she said.

"Well, it seems as though Candy called into work this morning and told this Dr. Franklin person that she was taking all of her accrued sick days *and* her two weeks' vacation and that he was to consider it her two weeks' notice. She quit!"

The stunning news sent a blow to Courtney's midsection. "Candy?"

"Yeah."

"My God, Nick, what did you do to her?"

"Me? Nothing. I didn't do a damn thing to her. At least, I don't think I did."

"Well, you must have done something." Suddenly the phrase "carpet lambada" flashed through Courtney's mind. "And I think I know what it was."

"What? Tell me."

"Candy called me yesterday," she said. "Actually, it was last night, after she had been with you all day. She told me that *it* happened again."

Nick hung his head, more out of overwhelming concern for Candace than outright shame. "It did. But I thought it was okay between us. If I hadn't thought it was okay, I wouldn't have started anything. I would have let her alone, believe me. And when it was over, everything felt so right. She didn't try to run away like a frightened rabbit like she did the first time. She stayed awhile. We talked. A good talk, I thought.''

"Obviously, you thought wrong." Courtney slipped off the bar stool and opened her refrigerator, pulling out a bottle of wine. She reached into a cabinet, got two glasses, and emptied the bottle's contents into the them. She didn't know about Nick, but at this point, she needed a drink, the stronger the better.

Both drank in silence until the glasses were empty.

"What do you think I ought to do?" he asked. "Phone the police and report her missing?"

"No, you can't file a missing-persons report until she's been gone for forty-eight hours."

"I thought it was twenty-four hours."

"No, forty-eight," she said. "They changed it. And even if you do file a missing-persons report, I doubt it will do you any good."

"Why do you say that?"

"Because Candy's over twenty-one. She a grown woman with a mind of her own, and if she wants to get so lost that nobody can find her, well, that's her right. The police can't force her to come home; it's against her constitutional rights."

"Damn. Damn, damn, damn!" Nick buried his face in his hands. "I wish to God I knew what I did. I'd take it back. I'd take it all back."

Enlightenment came slowly for Courtney. "Maybe you didn't do anything. Maybe it's Candy who did something."

"Like what?"

"Well, it's only a guess, mind you, because I'm not sure, but she might have finally gotten in touch with Don."

More blood drained from Nick's already pale face. His palms grew cold and damp. "Don?"

Courtney nodded. "That's who she said she was going to go see last night. It was the last thing she said to me when we spoke on the phone, as a matter of fact."

Nick couldn't avoid the sinking feeling in the pit of his stomach, the feeling that he might have already lost Candace. If she had gone to see Don as Courtney suggested, and if they had made up, then he stood no chance at all of ever getting her back. Not that he'd ever had her in the first place, he thought with a silent humorless chuckle. Her loyalties had always been with the other man in her life, and he knew it—he *had* known it from the very beginning.

Seeing the expression on Nick's face and interpreting it as despondency, Courtney dropped a comforting arm around his shoulders. "Come on, don't give up hope yet. I don't know for certain that she did go to Don."

"But if she did, and if she told him what we did and asked his forgiveness, there's a strong possibility that he forgave her. I know I would. And if Don did forgive her, you know what that means, don't you?"

"It doesn't mean a thing, Nick. For your own state of mind, stop jumping to all these wild conclusions."

"My mind? What mind is that, Court? After the day I've just spent, what little mind I had left is just about shot. I'm frantic."

"I know you are."

"I've got to find Candy and get this stupid misunderstanding between us straightened out."

"We'll find her." Eventually, Courtney thought. Candace, she knew, couldn't stay missing forever. She had to turn up sooner or later. And for Nick's sake, she prayed it was sooner.

"How?" Nick asked. "Do we call up Don and ask him where she is?"

"No, we don't do that. I don't have his number, and I don't think he's listed. We're going to have to go over to his place and find out."

"Oh, great. Just what I need on top of everything else—a face-to-face confrontation with Candy's boyfriend. The guy'll probably punch my lights out."

"Not Don. He's not the physical type."

Courtney placed the two now-empty glasses in the sink. "But first I think we should drop by Candy's."

"What for? I've already told you she's not at home."

"We don't know that for sure. It might be that she's just not answering her phone. She's done that before, when she felt like being left alone."

"But how do we get into her place? I've got to be honest with you, after the day I've just had, I don't think I'm up to breaking and entering."

"We won't have to do that." Courtney opened a drawer, rummaged around inside it for a moment, and finally produced a key. "She gave this to me the last time she went out of town. I was supposed to water her houseplants for her."

"Candy doesn't have any houseplants."

"I know. Every time she buys one, it dies on her, for some reason. But that's another story. We'll just let ourselves in with this key, check around the apartment, and let ourselves out again. No one will ever know the difference."

"They won't, huh?" Nick followed Courtney out of the kitchen and into the darkened hall. "Can I quote you if we get arrested by the cops?"

"Stop worrying. We're not going to get arrested." Courtney collected her purse and car keys on the table by the door, where she had dropped them when she first came in, and let herself out of the house, locking the door behind her. "But if by some slim chance we should have a close encounter with the security staff at Candy's apartment complex, I know a terrific lawyer who can bail us out of jail."

"That's what I like—a woman who thinks ahead," Nick muttered as he followed Courtney to his truck.

Much later, as they climbed the stairs to Candace's third-floor apartment, Nick took frequent glances over his shoulder, looking for some sign of a security guard. He half expected one to pop out of the shadows at any moment, brandishing a gun and yelling, "Freeze! You're under arrest!"

He gave his head a rapid shake. He'd been watching too many old detective shows on late-night TV.

"Here we go," Courtney said as she inserted the key into Candace's lock and opened the door. "And here we are. See, now wasn't that easy?"

Nick slipped into the apartment behind her, quickly closing the door. "Yeah, easy. Remind me not to take up a life of crime. My heart wouldn't stand the strain."

"Relax. We're not breaking and entering. If anybody hears us and reports us, we just tell the security staff that we're here to check up on Candy's things. Which, from the looks of it, seem to be still intact."

She wandered through the tiny living room, glancing at the photographs on top of the tables, the books and records and videotapes on the shelves. In the kitchen she opened cupboards, taking inventory of the dishes and pots and pans.

"No," she said, "nothing's missing."

"Nothing except Candy."

He flipped on the light switch in the bedroom and let Courtney precede him. They searched through the dresser drawers and closets, finding Candace's usual assortment of clothes hung and neatly folded.

"Her weekend suitcase isn't here," Courtney said. "And neither are her nightgown and bathrobe. I'll bet if we check out the bathroom, we'll find that some of her makeup and toiletries are missing, too."

"What are you saying, that she's skipped town?"

"I don't know if that's the exact phrase I would choose, but it's close, yes."

"That doesn't make sense," Nick said. "If she were going to run away for good, why would she take just some of her stuff with her and leave the rest of it behind?"

"Because she's not gone for good, silly. She took just enough of her things to last her a few days."

"A few days, huh?" God, Nick thought, could he last that long without her?

And then he had another thought, one that made him sick inside. "Do you think she and Don might have"— he swallowed the knot of fear in his throat—"eloped?"

"It's possible. Where Candy's concerned, just about anything is possible. But I seriously doubt it. The word 'elope' is not in her vocabulary. She's always wanted a big wedding, like the one Elise and Tony had."

Courtney led the way out of the bedroom, back into the living room, and headed for the front door. Nick, not knowing what else to do, followed her, turning out the lights behind them.

"Where to now?" he asked. "Don's?"

"Yep," Courtney said. "Let's just pray that he can shed some light on this little mystery of ours."

* * *

They arrived at Don's town-house apartment just as he was walking out his front door, a rather large suitcase in one hand and what looked to Nick like a plane ticket in the other.

"Son of a bitch," he mumbled as Courtney opened the door and climbed down out of the truck.

At that moment Don looked up, an expression of pleased surprise crossing his features as he recognized Courtney. But when he noticed the pickup truck she was getting out of, his expression changed to one of confusion. He had never thought of her as the pickup-truck type.

"Court? What are you doing here?" And then he saw Nick, circling the cab. "Hi, nice to see you again. Nick, isn't it?"

"Hi?" Nick said, stalking toward him. "That's all you gotta say to me, hi?"

"Calm down, Nick," Courtney said. "Let me handle this."

But Nick was too angry to hear her. "Where is she?" he demanded, grabbing Don by the lapels of his coat and pulling him bodily off the sidewalk so that their eyes were even. "What are you planning to do with her? Run off to Vegas or Reno or someplace like that and get married?"

"Put me down," Don said, feeling more ridiculous than frightened. "I don't know what you're talking about. And I certainly don't know *who* you're talking about."

"Candy, you pencil-necked geek. That's who we're talking about."

Alarmed by this new and not-too-pleasant side of Nick's personality, Courtney placed a hand on his arm. "Let him go."

"No, not until he tells us where Candy is."

"Nick, let him go," she said a bit more forcefully. "He can sue you for assault."

"Assault? I haven't assaulted him yet, but I'm seriously thinking about it. I'm gonna assault him all over this damn sidewalk if he doesn't tell me what the hell has happened to Candy."

"I don't know what's happened to her," Don said.

"Yeah, sure you don't."

"I don't! The last time I saw her was last night. She came over here, we talked, and then she left."

"I think he's telling the truth, Nick."

"Then why the suitcase?" Nick asked, glaring at Don. "You thinking about going somewhere?"

"Yes, I am. Florida."

Nick frowned and looked at Courtney. "Is this something new I don't know about—eloping to Florida?"

"Elope?" Don's voice broke in anxious concern. "I'm not eloping. I'm going to visit my mom and dad and sister. They all live there."

"Nick, listen to what he's saying," Courtney said. "He's not eloping with Candy. He's going to Florida. By himself."

As her words finally sank into Nick's enraged thoughts he slowly loosened his grip on Don's coat, letting the man drop to the pavement. "Is that true?"

"Why would I lie?" Now free, Don stepped back to safe distance, shifting his shoulders inside his wrinkled coat as one hand straightened his tie.

"Then where the hell is Candy?"

"I don't know," Don said. "It's like I told you before, the last time I saw her was last night."

"What time did she leave?" Courtney asked.

"Leave?" Don frowned, thinking, trying to recall the

events of the night before. "Oh, I don't know. Seven or eight o'clock, I guess. Something like that. I know I hadn't been home very long."

"Did she say anything to you about where she might be going after she left you?"

"No, not a word. Why, what's wrong? What's happened?"

"Candy's missing," Courtney said. "She called in to work this morning and quit her job. We just came from her apartment and know that she took a suitcase and some of her clothes, but we haven't a clue where she's gone."

"Good God!" Don said, appalled.

"Yeah, you can say that again," Nick said.

"When she was here last night, did she act as if she were upset?" Courtney asked.

"Yeah, at first she did," Don said. "But when she left she—well, if you want to know the truth, I had the feeling she was sort of relieved when she left. Probably because she broke up with me."

Nick took a step toward Don. "She what?"

Don stepped back. "She broke up with me. Why, is that bad?"

"No, that's good," Nick said, a smile slowly crossing his face. "That's very good."

"It means she finally made a decision," Courtney said. "The right one, I hope."

"You got any ideas where she might have gone?" Nick asked.

"No, none," Don said. "You said you checked her apartment?"

"Just a few minutes ago," Courtney said, "just before we came over here."

"And finding one of her suitcases and some of her

clothes gone, you naturally assumed that she and I were planning to run away together.'' Don nodded slowly, finally understanding the cause of Nick's earlier rage. ''Yeah, I can see where that might make you kind of mad, kind of irrational.''

Nick hung his head sheepishly. ''Sorry about that. Sorry about wrinkling your coat, too.''

''Forget the coat—it's all right,'' Don said. ''In your place, as worried as you are, I'd have probably done the same thing. I'm just glad you didn't decide to punch my lights out.''

''The notion had occurred to me,'' Nick said.

Don grinned. ''I know.'' He checked the time on his watch, and his smile faded. ''Look, I hate to have to cut this pleasant conversation short, but if I don't leave now, I'm going to miss my flight.''

''Then you'd better leave,'' Courtney said. ''Have a safe trip.''

''Will you two be okay?'' Don asked, heading for his car. ''Are you sure you don't want me to stick around awhile and help you locate Candy?''

''No, you go on,'' Nick said. ''We'll find her.''

''Eventually,'' Courtney added. ''She's bound to turn up sooner or later.''

And when she does, Nick thought, I'll wring her little neck for making me go through such hell.

♋ 14

CANDACE HAD NEVER FELT SUCH peace. She sat in an old lawn chair on her mother's patio, watching the sun slowly descend behind the trees and university buildings to the west. Warm breezes fluttered the full trees overhead, making the baby birds nesting in the branches chirp in high, shrill voices. She smiled. Why couldn't her life always be this calm?

"Candy, dinner's ready."

She turned and looked at the open back door, seeing her mother's smile at her. "What are we having?"

He mother shrugged. "Oh, nothing special. Fried chicken, mashed potatoes, green beans, corn bread, and peach cobbler."

"Sounds yummy. I wish you had let me help you."

"Allow another woman to come into my kitchen?" Her mother laughed. "I won't even let Lloyd or the boys help."

"Still, Mom . . ."

"Still nothing. Come inside and wash your hands.

We're going to eat as soon as Lloyd gets home. He's got Rusty's soccer game to coach tonight—if he can tear himself away from the English department early enough.''

Candace leaned forward, resting her elbows on the arms of the lawn chair. ''Have you got a minute?''

Her mother glanced back into the kitchen to make sure nothing was boiling over or burning on the stove, then she stepped out onto the patio, letting the screen door close behind her. ''For you? I've got more than a minute. What's the matter?''

''Oh, nothing really. I just thought we'd talk.''

The hollow aluminum legs of another lawn chair scraped across the concrete surface of the patio as her mother sat down beside her. ''That's all we've done for the past two days—talk. I thought you'd be talked out by now.''

Candace looked off into the distance, seeing nothing but well-tended fruit trees, her mother's small vegetable garden, and a fence that needed mending in a few places. ''You're happy here, aren't you?''

''Mmm, I could probably live a little further away from the campus. It can get awfully noisy here during football season. But yeah, I guess you could say I'm happy.''

''You love Lloyd a lot, don't you?''

''Candy, honey, I wouldn't have stayed married to the man for over twenty years if I hadn't loved him.''

''He's nothing like Daddy.''

Her mother hesitated. ''In some ways he is. In some ways he's not. After all, they're both men. But your daddy was a man driven by a frustrating need to create the masterpiece he believed he had in him. He still is frustrated. I don't think he'll ever be satisfied with his work, even though the work he does is very good.

"Lloyd, on the other hand, is a teacher. He's not driven by the inner demons that drive your father. He's just caught up in literature and long-dead poets and students who don't really care for English all that much, but who have to take his course so they can get a degree. And he's into making sure that Rusty's soccer team plays good enough this year to make it to the regionals. In other words, he's not quite as complex as your father."

"But he's still a good man."

"One of the best," her mother agreed.

She studied Candace for a moment, but couldn't read the thoughts going through her only daughter's head. "Does this have anything to do with that problem you've been having? Your *man* problem?"

Candace smiled. "Yes, I suppose it does."

"Want to tell me about it?"

"No, not really. No offense, Mom. It's not that I don't want to talk about it, it's just that this is one problem I've got to work out on my own. In fact, I've pretty much got most of it figured out." She reached over and took her mother's hand. "Thanks to you."

"Me?"

"Yes, you. Spending these last two days here with you and Lloyd and the kids has been wonderful. You've been a lot of help. More help than you could ever imagine."

"Thanks, I guess," her mother said skeptically.

"You're welcome." Candace slowly rose to her feet. "And now I think it's time I go back to Dallas. I think I'll leave right after supper."

"After supper?"

"Yes, I wouldn't want to miss your fried chicken and peach cobbler."

"But you can't leave now. You just got here."

"I know, but I have to go back sometime, Mom."

"Why couldn't you wait and leave in the morning, after breakfast? Good heavens, Candy, it's going to be dark soon."

"I know, but my car has headlights, and they're working. Besides, it's best that I get home."

"To this man problem of yours, right?"

"You got it."

Her mother heaved a heavy sigh and slowly stood up, walking with Candace into the kitchen. "When will we get to see you again? Not another four months like this last time, I hope."

"No, not that long. Maybe in another week or two."

"Do you know what you're going to do when you get back to Dallas?"

"Oh, yes. I've already got some plans made."

"Like what?"

"Well, the first thing Monday morning, I'm going job hunting. And this time I'm not going to settle for the kind of job that's boring, demeaning, or dehumanizing. I want something that's stimulating, challenging. I want a salary that's commensurate with the work I do. I want decent working conditions—no lab coats or chemicals. And I'd like to work with people who occasionally act like they're human beings and not a bunch of out-of-this-world slide-rules-for-brains rocket scientists."

"I can go along with that," said her mother. "And what about this problem man of yours? What are you going to do about him?"

Candace took a deep breath. "I'm not sure yet exactly. I've come up with one or two options, but we'll just have to wait and see which one I use."

"Sounds to me like you've really got your head on straight,"

"I think I do. I certainly hope so. It's about time. After all, I am twenty-seven now."

"So, you know what you want, huh?"

"I know what I don't want. I don't want to live my life in a vacuum anymore. I mean, I can tolerate the old nine-to-five grind because I know I have to. But the rest, as they say, is up to me. It's my choice."

Her mother wrapped an arm around her waist and hugged her close. "You'll let me know how it turns out, won't you?"

"Of course I will. You'll be the first to know."

"If I am," her mother said with a chuckle, "that'll be a first in itself."

"Well, maybe you won't be the absolute first. Maybe the one right after the first."

"The first being Courtney?"

"Yeah."

Her mother moved to the sink and washed her hands. "By the way, how is she doing these days? I haven't seen her in years."

"Oh, you know Court," Candace said. "She's the same as she's always been. Her law practice comes first and her private life comes second. A far distant second."

"She'd better get that straightened out and fast. If she doesn't, she's going to wake up one of these mornings and find that she's become an old woman who's living all by herself. I'm assuming, of course, that she does still live alone. She's not living with anyone, is she?"

"Who else would she live with?"

"I don't know. Some man, probably."

"No, no man."

"What about a cat or a dog?"

"No cat, no dog," Candace said. "Not even a bird or goldfish."

"But isn't there a man in her life?"

"Nope. She says she doesn't need one. She says that no woman really needs one."

"Maybe we don't, but they're certainly nice to have around, like when the weather's cold and your feet are cold, or a pipe bursts, or you're just plain lonely."

"I don't think Courtney gets lonely," Candace said. "She's far too busy to even think about it."

Her mother shook her head. "Must be nice to be so confident."

Two hours of driving separated Waco from Dallas. In daytime, familiar scenery helped to break the lonely monotony of Candace's solitary drive. But now, with the sunset turning the surrounding landscape from its late-spring green to an indistinguishable gray, she was left with nothing but her thoughts—her indecisive, troubled thoughts to keep her company.

The more she thought about her problem and the decision she knew she had to make, the more confused she became. Now that Don was out of the picture, it all hinged on Nick. Her future, his future—everything.

Should she go to him as soon as she got home, lay her cards on the table, and hope for the best? Or should she wait until morning to confront him? A good night's sleep would certainly help her broach the subject with him more clearly. But putting off the inevitable might cause her to lose some of her steam.

"Steam, hell. It's courage you need, McFarren."

Time sped by slowly as her car ate up the miles of interstate highway, first passing by Hillsborough and then Waxahachie. On the outskirts of DeSoto, the traffic began to grow more congested, the road more brightly lit with headlights and the red glow of taillights from the cars in front of her.

And then she saw the familiar Dallas skyline in the distance, its tall buildings illuminated against the dark sky. Home, she thought.

At a quarter of nine she drove through the gates of her apartment complex. An empty parking space in front of her building beckoned to her and tiredly she pulled into it.

Morning, she thought. I'll go see Nick in the morning.

15

"Have you seen those black-and-white storyboard layouts I did for the Adamson commercial?" Toby knelt on the floor beside Nick's drafting table, flipping through the stack of large drawings that rested there. He couldn't understand it. The man had a brand-new file cabinet just begging to be filled, but all he had in it was the pair of keys in a little plastic bag that had come with it.

Nick merely grunted and continued to stare morosely out of the window in front of him.

"I can't find them," Toby said. "I've looked everywhere, but they're gone."

"What's gone?" Nick asked woodenly.

Toby sighed. The man's file cabinet wasn't the only thing empty this morning, he decided. "The storyboard layouts for the Adamson dry cleaners' commercial we're supposed to start shooting next week," he said. "I need them. I know I saw them in here a couple of days ago. I had an idea, and I thought I'd change them, but now

I can't find them. Do you know where they are? Have you seen them?''

Toby, still on his knees, fell backward in alarm as Nick suddenly leaped to his feet, his chair turning over behind him, landing on the bare wood floor with a metallic clatter. "Good God!"

Startled by his employer's unexpected action, Toby muttered, "I hope that doesn't mean you threw them out. 'Cause we're sunk if you did."

"Threw what out, Tobe?" Nick said, a grin splitting his face.

"The Adamson—"

"Oh, them. They're somewhere over there on my desk. By the way, you did a great job on them, kid. Absolutely terrific. Remind me to give you a raise when I can afford it."

Toby remained on the floor, an expression of extreme befuddlement contorting his normally even features, as Nick raced out of the office. After a moment he nodded. "Those six cups of coffee he had this morning must've finally kicked in."

In the living room, Nick threw open the front door. Outside, halfway up the steps, Candace looked up and saw him.

"Hi," she said, letting her footsteps slow.

"Hi, yourself."

Where the hell have you been? Nick wanted to shout at her, but knew he didn't dare. She had come to him. After three days of not knowing where she was at or what she was doing or who she was doing it with, she had finally come to him. He would be grateful for that small amount of consideration, even if it killed him.

"How've you been?" she asked.

"Honestly?"

His clipped response surprised her. "Well, yes . . . honesty would be nice, I suppose."

"I've been kind of worried, that's how I've been. The question is, how have you been?" Nick gave himself a mental pat on the back for sounding so calm.

"I've been just fine. I went to Waco to visit my mother."

"Oh, Waco."

"Yeah." She started climbing the steps again. "You know where Waco is, don't you?"

"No, not really." And I don't give a damn, either, he thought. You should have been here with me.

"It's about a two-hour drive south of here."

Nick nodded, struggling to remain composed as she stepped onto his porch. "Well, how was it?"

"Nice," Candace said. "Very nice. I hadn't seen Mom in a couple of months, and I sort of missed her. Talking to her over the phone just isn't the same as talking to her face-to-face, you know. But then, I'm sure you know how that feels, living so far away from your parents in New York and all. It felt very good to be with her for a while."

"So, you were with your mom for the past three days." Three days, twelve hours, and fifteen minutes—give or take a few milli-seconds, he thought.

"Yeah."

Nick took a deep breath, the insincere smile on his face frozen in place. "You were with your mom in Waco, talking."

"Yes." Hearing the hollow sound of Nick's voice, Candace began to grow worried. "Is something the matter, Nick? Did I come over at a bad time?"

"Nooo! Whatever gave you that idea?"

"The way you're acting."

"How am I acting, Candy?"

"Like something's wrong."

"I don't know what could be wrong," he said, feeling the short leash on his composure snap in two. "I mean, I've been here for the past three days, wondering what the hell happened to you, worried sick that you might be lying dead in a ditch someplace, but other than that, everything's been just swell."

He was angry, and rightfully so, she realized. "I know, I should've called you."

"Damn right you should've. And if not me, then Court. We've been half out of our minds."

Candace blinked. "Courtney was worried about me?"

"Yes! Not as worried as I was, of course, but she was concerned enough to contact a friend of hers in the police department."

"Oh, no. You didn't report me missing, did you?"

"Almost. Not that it would have done us any good, according to Courtney, but we felt we had to do something."

"But I was fine. Nothing happened."

"Yeah, I know that now, but three days ago I didn't. I called you at home and couldn't get you. And when I called you at work, I was told you had quit your job. You had all but disappeared off the face of the earth. In a situation like that, it's only natural I assume something serious was wrong."

"You know I quit?"

"Yeah."

"Who told you?"

"I don't know—Shelly Something-or-other."

"Shelly Woods?"

"Yeah, I guess that's the name she said. At the time I really wasn't paying too much attention."

"How'd she find out?" Candace asked, more to herself than to Nick.

"From some guy named Franklin."

"Dr. Franklin? *My* Dr. Franklin?" Well, he wasn't exactly hers any longer, Candace realized. If anything, Dr. Franklin was now her ex.

"Yeah. It seems that your leaving left a rather sizable gap in his department, and he wasn't too thrilled with it."

Dr. Franklin had been upset? Candace smiled, wishing she had been at the office to see the normally cool, in-control scientist lose his composure and act like a human for once. It must have been an amazing sight.

Seeing Candace's smile, Nick resisted the urge to reach out and strangle her. "You think it's funny, turning people's lives upside down, do you?"

Instantly, her smile vanished. "No, of course I don't."

"Then what's with the grin?"

"I had an amusing thought, that's all. It was a private joke, all right?"

"No, it's not all right. It's anything but all right."

Witnessing the angry color that began to suffuse Nick's face, Candace had the distinct impression that once he unleashed his Italian temper, it might be hard for him to control it. It would certainly be a lot more than she could handle. Not wanting to be around for the event, if it should happen to occur, she turned slightly, intending to descend the front walk.

"Maybe I should come back later," she said, "when you're not so upset."

"You take one more step, and so help me God, I'll break your arm."

The husky tone of his voice challenged more than frightened her. "You'll what?"

"You heard me. I'll break your arm."

Tilting her chin, Candace drew forth all the composure she knew was slipping and gave him a very haughty, self-assured look. "No, you won't. You're not a violent man, Nick."

"You wanna bet? After the three days I've just lived through, violence is becoming almost second nature to me."

"Look, I know you're mad, but—"

"Honey, mad doesn't begin to describe the way I feel."

"Then calm down and tell me what word does describe it. Let's discuss this, but as civilized human beings, Nick, not bickering adversaries. I don't want to fight with you. That's not what I came here for."

"I don't want to fight with you, either. But I'm not going to talk about it here." He reached out behind him and opened the door. "Come inside and we'll talk."

Candace hesitated, her dubiousness clearly obvious.

"I won't touch you, if that's what you're worried about," he said. "I might yell so loud that the windows will rattle, but I promise I won't lay a hand on you."

"Honestly, Nick, I—"

"And we won't be alone, either," he said softly, angrily. "Toby's inside, working."

"Who's Toby?"

"My assistant. Now, will you stop cringing from me like a scared rabbit and come in?"

Candace girded up her courage and slowly entered the house. With only a few exceptions, the room looked no different from the last time she had seen it—the afternoon that she and Nick had made love on the floor in front of the couch. But it felt different—less cozy, less intimate.

As Nick closed the door behind them a young black

man emerged through the archway that led to the hall and the bedrooms beyond. He studied some drawings in his hands, then he looked up, saw Candace, and smiled.

"Hi," he said.

Candace smiled back. "Hi."

"Toby, Candy. Candy, Toby." Having done his social duty by introducing the strangers, Nick jerkily cocked his head a couple of times, silently telling Toby to make himself scarce.

Toby frowned, but he understood the message clearly. He had been on his way to the kitchen to get himself a drink, but that, he decided, would have to wait. "Well, I'd better get back to work. It's been nice meeting you."

"Nice meeting you, too, Toby."

"He's a good kid," Nick said as Toby vanished from sight. He scooped up a mound of newspapers and magazines from the couch and dropped them on the floor so that Candace would have an uncluttered place to sit.

"He seems like one. How long has he been working for you?"

"Two or three months. A couple of days after I moved in, he showed up on my doorstep, wanting a job." Nick shrugged. "I liked what I saw in his portfolio and hired him. It was probably the smartest thing I've done since I got here."

Candace felt a cold finger of fear crawl up her spine. "Meaning that all of the other things you've done have been stupid?"

Nick sat down beside her, slumping forward, letting his elbows rest on his knees. "Some things have been, some things haven't. It all depends on what we're talking about."

"How about we talk about me. You and me, specifically, Nick. Do I get pigeonholed with some of the stupid things you've done?''

He sighed deeply and turned his head to give her a long studied look. ''Why don't you answer that one, Candy. You seem to be more capable of it at the moment than I am.''

She opened her mouth and then closed it with a groan. ''Oh, damn, Nick, I don't know. Driving over here this morning, I had a pretty good idea what I was going to say to you. But now that I'm here, I'm a complete blank.''

''That's a start. Let's go with that.''

''With what?''

''Why you came here?''

''To talk to you, of course.''

''About what?''

''About us.''

''Is there an us, Candy? I know there's no longer a you and Don.''

''How did—''

''Court and I went to see him at his place. We were looking for you. We caught him just as he was about to leave for the airport. He stuck around long enough to tell us that you broke up with him.''

Candace issued an unamused snort. ''Some breakup. I suppose he told you what he told me—that there was never anything to break up, that there never had been.''

''Yeah, that's the impression I got.''

Sitting back with a dispirited sigh, Candace let her head fall onto the top edge of the couch and closed her eyes. ''I've made such a mess of things, trying to hold on to something that never even existed.''

''You and Don, you mean.''

''Yeah. I can't make that same mistake again.'' She

lifted her head to look at Nick. "I *won't* make it again. Life's too short."

"So, what are you going to do?" Better yet, he thought, who are you going to do it with, and am I included in the picture?

"Honestly?"

"Honestly."

"Well, for starters, I'm going to change jobs. And this time I'm not going to settle for the first place that'll hire me. I want to work for a company that's interesting, that has good benefits, halfway decent working conditions, and a good chance at advancement. I should be out there right now, pounding the pavement now, dropping off my résumés and putting in my application at places, but I thought I owed you an explanation first."

"And once you're gainfully employed again, then what?"

Candace swallowed the knot of trepidation in her throat. "Eventually, I want to get married and have a family."

Slowly, Nick nodded, hoping his expression didn't reveal the pleasure he felt inside. "Got anybody in mind for the position of husband?"

"Kind of." Her words came out soft and hesitant, her eyes unable to look directly at Nick.

"Anybody I know?"

What little composure Candace possessed vanished into thin air. "Oh, God, Nick, I don't want you to think that I consider you as some kind of consolation prize because I couldn't have Don. I don't, and you're not. You're grand-prize material. You probably deserve a grand-prize kind of wife. I don't know if that's how you think of me. A wife, I mean. You might have thought that way once, but that was some time ago."

"Yeah, I did. You've kind of put me through the wringer since then, though."

"I know, and I'm sorry. It's just that my life has been so messed up here of late. Well, longer than that, really. For the last few years, as a matter of fact. I mean, it was boring as hell in some respects, but in others it was still very messed up, you know? I didn't know what I was doing, or even why I was doing it. I just did what I did, believing that I was doing the right thing."

"And you were hating every minute of it," Nick said with an understanding nod. He had been in her shoes himself once. Before he had left the dog-eat-dog rat race of Madison Avenue, he had been certain that he was doing what he wanted, what was right for him. He had been killing himself for no good reason other than that he had thought it was expected of him. Now, of course, he knew differently.

"But then you came into my life," Candace said, "and you shook everything up. For the better, you understand. I know now that what you did at the time was good, not bad, and I appreciate it. Honestly, I do. You made me see that I was missing out on a lot—like living and not merely existing. Like finding and becoming the real me."

Nick nodded slowly. "So, as I understand it, what you're saying is, bottom line, you now think of me as husband material, is that it?"

Candace took a deep breath and prayed that she wouldn't regret what she was about to say. "Yes, I guess that's what I'm saying."

"All right," he said with a casual shrug.

Confused, she turned to look at him. " 'All right?' Is that all you have to say? I just told you I loved you."

"No, you didn't. Do you?"

"Do I what?"

"Love me?"

"Well, I wouldn't be sitting here, pouring out my heart to you, admitting all my past transgressions if I didn't."

"Then why don't you say it, Candy? I've said it to you, at least twice that I can recall."

With a studied frown Candace thought back, but came up empty. "No, you didn't."

"Oh, but I did."

"No, you did not, Nick. You never once said that you loved me. I know, because I would have remembered. All you said to me was that you were going to marry me, but that's all."

"It's the same thing, isn't it? At least, it is in my book."

"Well, it's not the same in mine. Not by a long shot, buster."

"Whoa. Why are you getting so defensive?"

"Because . . . telling me you're going to marry me sounds an awful lot like you're taking me for granted, like you expect me to thank you for it. Well, I'm not, Nick. I've been taken for granted enough for one lifetime."

"Actually, it was more of a case of my taking the situation for granted, not you," he said. "I mean, I knew I loved you the first time we were together. It just took you a little longer to realize it, that's all. But if you thought it sounded otherwise, then I'm sorry."

"You should b—" She broke off abruptly, her frustration fading in the face of surprise. "You knew you loved me that first night?"

"Yeah, strange as it may seem, I did."

"Why didn't you ever say anything?"

"Well, you know."

"No, I don't. Explain it to me."

"Because us guys just don't do that sort of thing. All our lives we've been taught to be all macho and tough so we can appear to be invulnerable to emotional pain— stuff like that, you know?" He inhaled a long breath and exhaled it slowly. "Besides, deep down, I guess you could say that I was afraid if I did tell you I loved you, I'd be running the risk of having history repeat itself on me."

"How would telling me you loved me do that?" Candace suddenly realized what he was trying to tell her. "Are you saying that it's happened to you before?"

"Yes, twice. You're not the only one who's been hurt by somebody you cared a lot about—or thought you cared a lot about. In my case it happened to be two somebodies."

"Oh, Nick, I'm sorry."

"Don't be. I'm not. I was, back when it happened, sure, but I got over it. That's why I didn't tell you I loved you. I didn't want it to happen to me again. You know, have a fling with you, knowing it was something special to me, then spill my guts out to you and have to watch you go back to Don. I don't like being dumped, Candy. I don't like being hurt."

"Neither do I. It's a bummer, isn't it?"

"You're telling me."

"So you decided to cut right to the chase."

"Yeah. I figured the straightforward approach was the way to go. After all, the standard hearts-and-flowers routine hadn't worked too well before. And besides, it's more suitable for the younger, more romantic guys."

Younger, more romantic guys? Candace smiled. "But you sent me flowers, Nick. In fact, you sent them twice. And balloons."

He grinned sheepishly. "Well, sometimes it's hard to break bad habits."

Following her instincts rather than protocol, she leaned over and wrapped her arms around his neck. "Habits like those aren't bad. Feel free to break them at any time."

"Promise you won't get mad at me when I do?"

She raised her right hand. "I promise."

He looked at her mouth. Her lips, almost bare of the pale pink lipstick she had applied earlier that morning, smiled at him so temptingly that he didn't think he could control himself. "Know what I'd like to do right now?"

"What?"

"I'd like to kiss you."

"If you're asking for my permission, go for it."

"I'd better not."

"Why not? What's stopping you?"

"Toby," Nick said. "He's working down the hall, remember?"

"So, we can be quiet, can't we?"

"Well, we could, but you know what kissing always leads to with us."

Candace grinned. "Yeah, the carpet lambada."

"The what?"

"You'll have to ask Courtney for a definition," she said, pulling his face closer to hers. "She's the one who coined the phrase."

Many silent moments later, Nick suddenly yelled out, "Toby!"

Another moment passed, and Toby appeared in the archway. "Yeah, whatcha need?"

"I need you to take the rest of the day off. You've worked hard enough."

"What are you talking about?" Toby asked. "It's

not even ten o'clock yet. I've barely gotten started on those—''

"Never mind," Nick said, handing him ten dollars. "Go see a movie or have an early long lunch or something. The rest of the day's on me."

Toby studied the crisp bill in his hand, and then he looked up and saw the rosy expression on Candace's face. Well, he thought, getting ten dollars to get lost was enough incentive for him.

"You want me to come back this afternoon?"

"No, tomorrow morning will be okay," Nick said, gazing longingly at Candace. "Better yet, make it the day after tomorrow."

"Right, gotcha." Toby nodded and headed for the door. "Y'all be cool." Fat chance of that happening, he thought, grinning as he closed the door behind him.

ᕲᕱ 16

COURTNEY MOANED IN FRUSTRATION as her phone rang. She had left explicit instructions with her secretary not to be disturbed unless it was absolutely essential. Obviously, this call must be important or Alicia wouldn't be ringing through, but she would rather not have to take it. She was almost finished with the Bryant contract and wanted nothing more than to get it out of the way. But fate seemed to have other plans, she realized, slipping off a large gold button earring as she reached for the receiver.

"Yes, what is it, Alicia?"

"Sorry to bother you, but your friend Miss McFarren is on line two."

"Candy? Thanks." Courtney punched one button on her phone, disconnecting Alicia, then she punched another, connecting her with Candace. "Well, it's about time. Where the hell have you been for the past week? Nick and I have been worried sick. We looked all over town for you."

The hesitant chuckle that came through the receiver angered Courtney.

"Good afternoon to you, too, Court. Or should I call you Grumpy? You sure sound like it."

Gritting her teeth, Courtney groped mentally for an acerbic comeback, but couldn't think of one. Candace would be grumpy and out of sorts, too, if she had spent the week of near-sleepless nights that Courtney had. But obviously Candace hadn't; she sounded much too chipper and well rested.

"So where were you?" she asked.

"Waco," Candace said. "I went to see Mom."

"Your mother, huh?" Why hadn't she thought of that? When Nick had told her about Candace's disappearance, her first thought had been of Candace winging her way to some remote tropical paradise. Or, closer to home, lying dead in a rural drainage ditch.

"Yeah, she lives there, remember?"

"Yes, I remember," Courtney said. "I just wish you had told someone where you were going before you left."

"I'm over twenty-one. I didn't think it was necessary to account to everyone for my whereabouts."

Inconsiderate wasn't a word Courtney normally associated with Candace, but it looked as though things were changing. And not for the better.

"Okay, fine," she said. "You were in Waco. Are you still there?"

"No, I'm at home. I just dropped by for a minute to get a few things."

"Don't tell me you're thinking of leaving town again?"

"No, I'm here for good this time."

Thank God for that, Courtney thought, staring at her office ceiling.

"The reason I called . . ." Candace began.

"Yes?"

"Well, I was wondering if you were doing anything this evening?"

At that moment Courtney's outer door opened and David Ballard walked in, his coat discarded, his shirt sleeves rolled up his forearms, and his glasses perched halfway down his nose as he perused the thick sheaf of papers in his hand.

"About this last paragraph," he said.

Courtney covered the receiver with her hand. "I'll be with you in just a minute."

David looked up, saw that she was on the phone, and nodded, telling her he understood. As she returned to her phone call he sauntered over to a chair and sat down, his attention reverting to the documents he held.

"As a matter of fact, I think I am doing something," Courtney said. "I may have to work late."

"Darn," Candace said.

"Look, I hate to be abrupt, but I'm sort of tied up at the moment. Is there any particular reason why you called?"

"Yes, I wanted you to come to dinner tonight."

"Dinner?" Courtney couldn't believe her ears. Candace had been gone for almost a week, and now that she had decided to breeze back into town all she could think of was having dinner? What about Nick? Had she called him? Had she put the poor guy out of his misery yet? Or was she planning to keep him dangling until he succumbed to extreme anxiety?

Eyeing David, and knowing that he could hear at least her end of the conversation, Courtney suppressed her flaring temper.

"Yeah, dinner," Candace said. "You do intend to

take a dinner break and eat sometime tonight, I hope.''

"At some point, yes, I suppose I will. But I can't get away and meet you tonight. And even if I could, I've got to go home and start packing. I'm leaving for San Francisco the day after tomorrow.''

"Oh, San Francisco!" Candace said. "The deal you've been working on for Mr. Bryant finally went through?''

"Not yet. We won't know for sure until we get there.''

"We?''

Courtney glanced over at David. They made eye contact, and she held up a finger, assuring him that she wouldn't be too much longer. Watching him go back to his documents, she covered the mouthpiece with her hand and lowered her voice. "David Ballard's going with me.''

"No kidding? Is he there in your office with you now?''

Now you're catching on, Sherlock, Courtney thought. "Yes, as a matter of fact.''

"Okay, well I guess I'll call you lat—no, wait a minute. Why don't you ask him to come tonight, too.''

"To dinner?'' Courtney asked.

"Sure, why not?''

"I don't think so." Courtney knew that the less she exposed her boss to her quirky friend, the better off he would be. The better off she would be, too. Making good impressions with the upper echelon was bound to pay off in the long run, and one of these days she wanted her name on the company letterhead.

"Oh, come on, Court. The two of you can't work all night. You've got to take a break at some time or other, don't you?''

"Well, yes, but—''

"Then why not meet us at the restaurant."

"Us?"

Candace's resultant giggle traveled through the receiver and into Courtney's ear, causing goose bumps to form on the back of her neck.

"Yes, Court. Us."

"Does the other part of your us involve Nick?"

"Yes."

Excitement raced through Courtney's veins. "Candy?"

"No, I'm not saying another word, so don't even ask. If you want to know any more, you're going to have to meet us in the French Room at the Adolphus at seven sharp."

"The French Room?" A flock of butterflies suddenly took flight in Courtney's stomach. She had only been to the French Room once in her life, and that had been years earlier. The prospect of getting to go there again was more tempting than she cared to admit.

"Seven sharp, you say?"

"That's right."

Courtney flipped open her Filofax, found she was free from six o'clock on, and made a notation, circling it in red. "I can't say about David, but I'll be there." A team of wild horses couldn't keep her away.

"You'd better be. 'Bye."

Ending her conversation with Candace, Courtney replaced the receiver and smiled at David. "I'm sorry about that."

"Oh, no problem," he said. "It gave me time to go over this last paragraph again."

Her excitement began to ebb, apprehension taking its place. "Is something the matter with it?"

"Nothing major. You might want to alter a minor point

in the few places I've circled in pencil, but that's all. Glance over it later and see what you think. You may decide not to change anything.'' He closed the long manila folder in his lap and slipped off his reading glasses. ''Looks like we'll be getting to go home earlier tonight than we expected.''

''Great! How about dinner?''

David's thick dark eyebrows rose in surprise as a pleased grin slowly appeared about his lips. ''Miss Ames, are you asking me for a date?''

''I'm asking you to dinner, yes. How does the French Room at the Adolphus sound?''

''It sounds very impressive. My, my, you certainly know how to show a man a good time.''

Courtney smiled sheepishly. ''Thank you, but you're complimenting the wrong lady. It's my friend Candy you should be thanking. She's the one who invited me. Well, us, actually.''

''Any particular reason for going to the French Room, or does she just enjoy spending lots of money?''

If he only knew, Courtney thought. Candace wasn't exactly the French Room type. McDonald's, yes, or any place that served through a drive-through window, but not someplace as classy and elegant as the Adolphus.

''I'm not sure,'' Courtney said as David rose to his feet, ''but I've got the strangest feeling that something's going on, or that something will be going on tonight. Something very important.''

He dropped the file on her desk. ''Sounds intriguing.''

''Intriguing enough to come to dinner with me and find out?''

''What time?''

''Seven.''

He nodded with a thoughtful frown. ''I'll have to check

my calendar, but I'm almost certain I can make it.''

She watched him as he walked out of her office, closing the door quietly behind him. Leaning back in her chair, she smiled. ''You do that, big boy. You do that.'' God, he was such a hunk.

The French Room was just as Courtney remembered it. The ceiling that soared a good twenty feet overhead was covered entirely in muted paintings of flora, fauna, and half-naked cherubs. Elaborately framed works of art graced the walls. Exquisite china, sparkling crystal, and silver sat atop each of the tables where well-dressed patrons dined in the regal-looking surroundings.

''It's like something out of a seventeenth-century French château, isn't it?'' she whispered to David as they stood in the entrance, waiting for the maître d'.

David eyed the magnificent artwork around him and above him and shook his head in amazement. ''Actually, I was thinking more on the line of something you'd find in an Old West bordello. But that's just my opinion, you understand.''

Courtney smiled. ''I take it you're speaking from experience?''

''About what?'' he countered, grinning. ''This place reminding me of a bordello, or that I just insinuated I'm old enough to have lived in the Old West?''

''Take your pick.''

''Contrary to how old I may look or, at the moment, how old I may feel, I'm only thirty-eight, Courtney. That's a bit too young to have come from the Old West.''

''What about the other?''

''The bordello?''

''Yes. Have you ever been to one?''

David cleared his throat as a faint blush appeared in

his cheeks. "That, Miss Ames, is none of your business."

The maître d' approached them with a smile. "Good evening."

"Good evening," David said. "We're with the Giulianni party. I believe we're expected."

"Ah, yes. They arrived a few moments ago. Would you follow me, please."

Weaving their way between the tables, they crossed to the tall windows on the opposite side of the room. Courtney took the opportunity to glance down at the tables to see what everybody was eating. Everything from the fish to the beef to the salad looked delicious.

She saw Candace and Nick look up as they drew near their table. Seeing their somewhat mischievous smiles, Courtney had to restrain herself from giggling like the teenager she had once been. If she had only suspected it before, she now knew for certain that Candace and Nick had made up. A good thing they had, she decided as she sat down across from Candace; she couldn't have taken much more of their squabbling. Neither, she suspected, could Nick, who looked more than just pleased with himself; he appeared ecstatically happy.

What she wouldn't give to be in Candace's shoes. To have someone like Nick love her as much as he loved Candace. Granted, they might be different as night and day, and would undoubtedly have their ups and down, but they were made for each other; she could see it in their faces and in the fact that they were holding hands under the table. That alone sent her positive vibrations soaring. She had a strong hunch that at some point during dinner they were going to announce their engagement. And when they did, she would restrain herself and not say "I told you so," or "It's about time." She would remain cool and elegant. She had to; David, her boss, was present.

"Glad to see you could make it, David," Nick said, standing and shaking David's hand.

"I'm glad you asked me to come along," David said. "The French Room has always been one of my favorite restaurants."

"You've been here before?" Candace asked.

"A few times," David said, taking his seat. "They were mostly for business dinners, though. You know, good food but sometimes-not-so-good conversation?"

"Well, no business tonight," Candace said. "Right, Nick?"

"Right," Nick said. "Tonight is strictly for relaxation and pleasure. Good food, good wine, good company—"

"And yummy desserts," Courtney said as a waiter wheeled a cart by their table. Obscene-looking high-calorie confections covered the cart. "I've got a feeling my diet's going to take a beating tonight."

"Mine too," Candace said, "but you're not going to hear me complain."

Their waiter presented each of them with leather-bound menus, and they spent some time perusing their options. Once they had made their selections, the waiter then conferred with Nick as to his choice of wines.

"The Chardonnay for the first and second courses, I believe," Nick said, "and, of course, champagne for dessert. Your finest vintage, if you please."

"Very good, sir." The waiter nodded and walked away.

"Champagne?" Courtney asked, trying to hide her amusement. Nick and Candace thought they were being so smart, acting so cool and unaffected. But she knew.

She had their number. "Is this evening a special occasion, or something?"

Nick nodded slowly. "Sort of. I like to think of it as something of a welcome-home party for Candy."

"Oh, have you been out of town?" David asked, lifting his glass of Evian and taking a sip.

"Yes, I have," Candace said. "I spent the earlier part of this week visiting with my mother."

"Where does she live?"

"Waco."

Candace's response so took David by surprise that he choked slightly on his water. "Waco?"

Smiling, Candace nodded.

"I'm sorry," David said. "I'm not making fun of Waco or anything. It's a great town. I know, I lived there for four years while I went to Baylor. It's just that I thought you had really been away, out of state. Maybe even out of the country."

"That's all right," Candace said. "No offense taken."

"Come on, you two, enough's enough," Courtney said, eyeing Nick and Candace. "This is a lot more than just a welcome-home party for Candy. You don't come to the French Room for something like that; you have beer and pretzels in your living room or margaritas and nachos at a bar on lower Greenville Avenue. What's really going on?"

"Later," Nick said.

"You're going to make us sweat it out?" Courtney asked.

"I promise that all will be revealed in good time, old friend," Nick said.

"Well, you may be revealing all later, but I'll bet I can guess right now," Courtney said.

"I'll bet you can't."

Candace's husky, secretive tone didn't faze Courtney. "Candy, it's obvious even to me that you and Nick have patched up your differences."

The couple in question traded glances, then looked back at Courtney and nodded.

"Yes, we've done that," Nick said.

"So, have you asked her to marry you yet, or what?" Nick merely grinned. "Later, Courtney."

"No, darn it, not later. Now."

"Courtney, I don't think you're going to get any more information out of them that way," David said. "You've got to be patient, subtle, play it cool."

"Patience is not and never has been my strong suit," she said.

"But I thought all lawyers knew how to remain cool under pressure," Nick said. "At least Perry Mason always is."

"I'm not Perry Mason," she said.

"I can attest to that," David said, lifting his glass of water in a mock salute.

"What David is trying to say," Courtney said, "is that I'm not very good in a tense courtroom situation. I never have been; that's why I practice corporate law instead of criminal law. I can't be cool. And after what these two have put me through this past week, I don't think I should have to be cool."

"What we've put *you* through?" Nick asked.

"Yes. She quits her job, runs off to Waco, doesn't tell anyone where she's going, and you drag me all over town looking for her. I probably haven't slept more than six hours since she disappeared."

"I didn't mean to make you worry, Court," Candace said. "Honest, I didn't."

"Then put me out of my misery. Give me a reasonable explanation."

"You'll get one," Candace said.

"Just not right now," Nick said, grinning.

"Yes, I know," Courtney said. "Later."

"That's right." Nick leaned back and draped an arm around Candace's chair, the smug look on his face infuriating Courtney.

🌀 17

Aᴌᴛʜᴏᴜɢʜ ᴅɪɴɴᴇʀ ʟᴀsᴛᴇᴅ ᴏɴʟʏ forty-five minutes, it seemed more like four hours to Courtney. During the appetizer, they chatted about the nation's economy and the threat of inflation. During the salad course, they touched briefly on unemployment. And during the main course, they got down to a really heavy discussion of environmental pollution and the feasibility of recycling.

Thank God for dessert, Courtney thought as the same waiter she had seen earlier wheeled the dessert cart over to their table.

"I've always been a pushover for chocolate," Candace said, eyeing a chocolate-hazelnut torte, iced with dark chocolate and decorated on top with white chocolate filigree swirls. "I'll have that, please."

The waiter smiled and served her up a slice.

"Courtney?" Nick asked.

"Give me a minute; I'm still trying to make up my mind." Let's see now, she thought. I'm about the same size as Candy, so I could probably strangle her with very little effort. But that wouldn't work on Nick. He's much too big. How dare they keep her waiting in suspense like this?

"Dave, what'll you have?" Nick asked.

"Everything looks so good," David said. "Is that raspberry cheesecake?"

"No, sir," the waiter said. "It's more like a raspberry trifle than an actual cheesecake. It's a specialty of the chef's, and very good."

"I'll trust your judgment," David said. "I'll have some."

The waiter smiled again and served him a generous helping.

"Courtney, are you ready yet?" Nick asked.

"In a minute," she said. If I can't strangle Nick, I'll do the next best thing. I'll stick a dagger in his heart. He had no right to look so smug.

"Well, then, I think I'll have some of that," Nick said, pointing at a multilayered loaf. "What is it?"

"Hazelnut sponge cake filled with layers of buttercream and topped with whipped cream and almonds," the waiter said, serving him a slice.

"Time's up, Courtney," David said. "It's your turn."

"I'll have the pecan pie," she said.

"Actually, it's bourbon pecan pie, miss," the waiter said, cutting her a slice. "Would you like some hard sauce on top?"

"Yes, please." Hard sauce, a very thin nylon cord, and a sharp knife, she added silently. She had had enough of this cat-and-mouse game of Nick and Candace's. She wanted an explanation, and she wanted it right now!

But she had to wait. The wine steward brought over the bottle of champagne that Nick had ordered and spent an inordinate amount of time opening the bottle and pouring it into each of their fluted champagne glasses.

Once the glasses were all filled and the waiter departed, Nick lifted his glass in a toast. "To good food, good conversation, and last but not least, to very good friends." He eyed Courtney and gave her a wink.

She wanted to sneer at him, but instead she smiled politely and she sipped her champagne.

"Now it's my turn," David said, lifting his glass and turning slightly to face Courtney. "To a long hard job well done, to the lady who did most of the work, and to her success in San Francisco. May you rake in the bucks."

"Oh, I'll drink to that," Courtney said.

She took a sip, then lifted her glass again, deciding it was time for Nick and Candace to pay the piper. "To Nick," she said, "who so thoughtfully invited us tonight and who's footing the bill for this little extravaganza. And to Candace, who, it seems, after twenty-seven years, has finally learned to keep a secret. A secret, by the way, which isn't very secret at all."

"Secret?" Candace asked, her blue eyes twinkling. "I'm not keeping any secrets."

"Yes, you are," Courtney said. "You've kept your left hand hidden in your lap all evening, and I'll bet I can guess why. It's got an engagement ring on it, doesn't it? A modest little diamond set in gold."

Still keeping her left hand out of sight, Candace looked down at her lap and slowly shook her head. "No, there's no engagement ring on it."

"There's got to be," Courtney said.

"Sorry, Court, but there's not."

"You mean, Nick hasn't asked you to marry him? After all he's been through—what am I saying? After all

I've been through for him and for you, he still hasn't asked you to marry him? Why not, Nick?''

Nick shrugged. ''It's not my fault. I offered to buy her an engagement ring, I even had a couple in my price range picked out for her to choose from, but she said she didn't want one.''

''That's right, I don't,'' Candace said.

Courtney sat back in her chair with a dispirited grunt. ''That's the stupidest thing I've ever heard. Every woman wants an engagement ring.''

''Not me,'' Candace said.

Courtney could see that Candace was fighting hard to keep a straight face, and that Nick was already grinning from ear to ear, and it aroused her curiosity even more. ''But he did offer to get you one.''

''Yes,'' Candace said.

''Then he *did* ask you to marry him.''

''No, he didn't. If you must know, he told me.''

''Asking you, telling you, what's the difference? It's the same thing,'' Courtney said, feeling more frustrated with each passing second.

''No, it's not,'' Candace said.

''Yes, it is.''

''May I interrupt?'' David said.

''I wish you would,'' Nick said, his voice laced heavily with amusement.

''Courtney, I think you're missing something here,'' David said. ''Something that's very apparent even to me, and I'm just an outsider.''

''Like what?'' she growled.

''Like the fact that—'' David broke off and shook his head. ''Oh, never mind. You tell her, Nick.''

''Please do,'' Courtney said. ''Somebody please tell me something.''

Nick cleared his throat. "Well, I guess we've strung her along long enough. You may as well show her, Candy."

Slowly, Candace lifted her left arm, her hand emerging into view.

It took Courtney only a moment to see the circle of diamonds on the third finger of her friend's left hand.

"My God," Courtney said. "You're married?"

Candace nodded, tears of happiness stinging her eyes.

"When?" Courtney had never felt more stunned in her life. Stunned, surprised, pleased more than she could say, and just a little bit hurt.

"This morning," Candace said.

"We decided to forgo all the usual fancy-shmancy church stuff," Nick said. "That's not for us. We wanted something small and private."

"And quick," Candace added.

"Yeah," Nick said. "Oh, not for the reason you might think. We're going to wait awhile before we decide to bring any little Giuliannis into the world. The fact is, I didn't want to wait too long. Planning a big wedding takes time, and I didn't want Candy changing her mind."

"Ellie almost changed her mind, remember?" Candace asked.

"But why didn't you tell me?" Courtney asked. "I mean, I thought I was your best friend. Aren't best friends supposed to tell each other things like this?"

"I wanted to, but it's like Nick just said, Court. We didn't want anything big and elaborate, like Ellie and Tony's wedding. And besides, we had already made up our minds, so why put it off?"

"To let your friends celebrate with you," Courtney said. "Getting married is special, you need to share it with the people you love."

"It's also personal," David said, drawing a mind-your-own-business look from Courtney. "But hey, that's just an outsider's opinion."

Courtney reached across the table and captured Candace's hand in hers to study the ring more closely.

"It's beautiful," she said.

"Thanks," Candace said. "Nick picked it out. All by himself. He has such good taste, don't you think?"

"Yes," Courtney said, giving Nick a stern look, "but it would look twice as beautiful with an engagement ring in front of it. Something, say, one or two karats and pear-shaped."

"When I'm rich," Nick said. "Until then, she'll just have to make do with this."

"Yes, we're working on a very limited budget," Candace said.

"With only one income between the two of you, you can say that again," Courtney said. "You are going to look for another job soon, I hope?"

"That offer of coming to work for our law firm still holds," David said.

"Thanks, but I've already got a job," Candace said.

"You do?" Courtney asked.

"Yes, I do."

"Doing what?"

"Oh, the same thing I did before—secretarial work."

"For whom?" Courtney asked.

Candace smiled, her face glowing with a long-sought peaceful inner happiness as she gestured to her husband. "Court, I'd like you to meet my new boss."

18

"WHATEVER ELSE WE DO IN THE next fifty or so years of our marriage, we'll never be able to top what happened tonight," Nick said later that evening as he lay beside Candace in their four-poster bed. Soft light from the lamp atop Nick's bedside table turned the room's starkness into a cozy cocoon. "Did you see the look on Court's face when you told you you were working for me."

"I thought I was working with you, darling, not for you. Equal partners, you said, remember?"

"Of course," he said, turning onto his side and snuggling close to her. "My error. I'm sorry."

"She looked even more surprised when I showed her my ring." Surprised, shocked, and from the way Courtney had acted a little bit hurt. "You know, Nick, maybe we should have told her, let her be a part of it."

"No, we shouldn't have, either," he said, his voice quiet but firm.

"Why not? She's my best friend. Yours too, consid-

241

ering how the two of you plotted and connived against me.''

"We did no such thing."

"Yes, you did. I'll bet you were on the phone with her at least three times a day, planning little strategies, setting your devious traps.''

"Nah, not three times."

Candace heard what he didn't say as well as what he did say. She tilted her head on Nick's furry chest and looked up at him. "Once a day?''

"Yeah, that sounds about right." A fist jabbed him softly in the ribs, causing him to grunt. "And I still say we did the right thing by not telling her.''

"How can you say that?''

"Easy. Remember what happened when you and Court started meddling into Ellie and Tony's wedding plans? They almost decided to call it off.''

"That wasn't the reason. Tony got that big promotion and was transferred back to New York. That's what almost broke them up. It had nothing to do with Court and me helping Ellie. Besides, she deserved a big wedding.''

"Are you saying you didn't?''

Hearing the faint note of regret in Nick's voice, Candace snuggled closer to him. "I didn't want one," she said. "There's a difference.''

"Why didn't you want a big wedding?''

"Oh, I don't know. I guess, for one thing, big weddings take too much time to plan and get organized. And then there's all the expense. Neither one of us could have afforded a big wedding, and we both know it. I didn't have a job—''

"You have one now.''

"Yes, I know, but I'm not earning very much. In fact, I haven't earned a dime, because my wonderful, sexy boss has a very limited income. And while I know that's bound to change in the near future, the fact remains that at the moment, we're both the same as broke.''

"You can say that again."

Nick held her close, the fingers of his hand running up and down her arm, feeling the silky-smooth flesh.

"Are you sorry?" he asked after a moment.

Sorry? she wondered. "About what?"

"Marrying a guy with no money?"

"It wasn't your net worth that I was attracted to, Nick." She bent her knee, letting it glide up his thigh to a most sensitive masculine area on his body. When it reached its goal, she gently nudged him. "It was you, you big sexy beast."

"Watch it, Candy. If your knee keeps that up, we're going to be adding new members to the Giulianni clan much sooner than we planned."

"Would that be so bad?"

"No, but I'd rather we wait."

Recognizing the sense of his words, and agreeing with him, she lowered her knee slowly to a safer, less compromising distance.

"One of these days," he said, "I'm going to give you everything you've ever wanted or dreamed of having. A closetful of new clothes, a big house in the suburbs, a new car every year, lots of kids . . ."

"I'll settle for two kids, thank you," she said. "No more than three. And I don't need a new car every year. One every other year, or every three years will suit me just fine. As for a lot of clothes—I'm not a clothes hound. A new outfit occasionally is all I need. And the big house would be very nice, but . . ."

"But what?"

"Well, do you know what I'd really love to have more

than anything else in the world?''

"Name it, baby, it's yours. Or it will be, as soon as I can afford it.''

"A maid,'' Candace said. "Can I have a maid, Nick? I'll work for you for free, for years if necessary, if you'll promise to get me a maid. I hate housework.''

He tilted her face up to his and lowered his mouth to hers. "A maid it is. You got it, Candy.''

When their kiss ended, they snuggled closely again, each feeling, loving the other's warmth and nearness.

Then suddenly Candace stiffened and back away.

"What?'' Nick asked.

"When Court and I went to the powder room . . .''

"Yeah.''

"She told me all about what happened the day you two went to Don's, looking for me.''

"Yeah, so?''

"So, would you have really duked it out with him like some barbaric Neanderthal just to win my hand?''

"Win your hand?'' Nick laughed. "Baby, getting possession of your ten fingers wouldn't have been enough. I wanted all of you.''

"Stop it. You know what I'm saying.''

"Yeah, I know.''

"Well, would you have fought him if he hadn't told you we'd broken up?''

"The idea had crossed my mind, sure. But as it turned out, punching his lights out wasn't necessary. We settled our differences like two civilized human beings.''

"Mmm!''

To Nick, Candace's murmur sounded like the purr a contented cat might make. "What's that 'mmm' for?''

"Oh, nothing in particular.''

"Then be general. What was the 'mmm' for?''

"Well, I know you didn't fight for me, but I still like the idea of you thinking about doing it."

"That's what I thought."

"No one's ever fought for me before."

"I will," he said, burying his nose into the feathery tresses at the top of her head. "I'll slay dragons for you."

"There aren't any dragons these days, Nick."

"Lucky them." He kissed her again, longer this time, and with a lot more passion. "Are you happy?"

"I'm ecstatic, Nick, and I didn't think I ever would be. I'm happy with the way my life is finally turning out, the way my future looks . . . and I'm very happy with you."

"Then what do you say we turn the lights out and celebrate a little. It's not every day we get married."

With a little giggle, Candace reached across him and flipped off the switch. "Let the games begin."

From the *New York Times* bestselling author
of <u>Morning Glory</u> and <u>Bitter Sweet</u>

LaVyrle Spencer

One of today's best-loved authors of bittersweet
human drama and captivating romance.

___THE ENDEARMENT	0-515-10396-9/$4.95
___SPRING FANCY	0-515-10122-2/$5.95
___YEARS	0-515-08489-1/$5.95
___SEPARATE BEDS	0-515-09037-9/$5.99
___HUMMINGBIRD	0-515-09160-X/$5.50
___A HEART SPEAKS	0-515-09039-5/$5.50
___THE GAMBLE	0-515-08901-X/$5.95
___VOWS	0-515-09477-3/$5.99
___THE HELLION	0-515-09951-1/$5.95
___TWICE LOVED	0-515-09065-4/$5.99
___MORNING GLORY	0-515-10263-6/$5.99
___BITTER SWEET	0-515-10521-X/$5.95